LAY YOUR ARMOR DOWN

ALSO BY MICHAEL FARRIS SMITH

Salvage This World

Nick

Blackwood

The Fighter

Desperation Road

Rivers

The Hands of Strangers

LAY YOUR ARMOR DOWN

MICHAEL FARRIS SMITH

LITTLE, BROWN AND COMPANY

New York Boston London

Little, Brown and Company
Hachette Book Group
1290 Avenue of the Americas, New York, NY 10104
littlebrown.com

First Edition: May 2025

Little, Brown and Company is a division of Hachette Book Group, Inc. The Little, Brown name and logo are trademarks of Hachette Book Group, Inc.

The publisher is not responsible for websites (or their content) that are not owned by the publisher.

The Hachette Speakers Bureau provides a wide range of authors for speaking events. To find out more, go to hachettespeakersbureau.com or email hachettespeakers@hbgusa.com.

Little, Brown and Company books may be purchased in bulk for business, educational, or promotional use. For information, please contact your local bookseller or the Hachette Book Group Special Markets Department at special.markets@hbgusa.com.

Book interior design by Marie Mundaca

ISBN 9780316573375
LCCN 2024949128

1 2025

MRQ-C

Printed in Canada

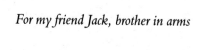

For my friend Jack, brother in arms

There is only one day left, always starting over:
it is given to us at dawn and taken away from us
at dusk.

—*Jean-Paul Sartre*

NIGHT

1

She moved in the solemn lamplight of the cluttered house like the vague figure of a troubled dream. She shuffled from room to room, opening drawers and closet doors and picking up things and putting them into the grocery sack. No sense or order in the gathering. A random ring and a broken bracelet from a spilled jewelry box. One shoe. A ragged notebook from the bottom of a stack of other ragged notebooks. Two postcards from a longdead sister. A handful of hairclips. A small wooden picture frame that held the rudimentary drawing of an angel that had been created by her child decades before.

She wore a thin housecoat that hung on her aged and slender figure. Her gray hair in a matted mess. She talked to herself as she moved throughout the house. Reminding herself of errands that had been years ago completed and gossiping about people she no longer knew and singing fragments of songs that had once played on the radio during the summer days of her smalltown youth. In doorways she would stop and look into the shadows and touch the tip of her index finger to her chin and hold it there in troubled thought and then she would begin again to fill the sack with the random fragments of time gone by.

At the end of the hallway the closet door was open and the contents overflowed and spilled out onto the floor as if the house was regurgitating its own clutter. The pace of her rambling quickened as she dropped to her knees and began to dig into the closet as if just remembering something essential. Her arms thin and weak but working in a sudden fever as she pushed away dirty towels and newspapers and shoeboxes and she burrowed into the closet. At the bottom of the pile she found a red tin coffee can and she opened the top and felt inside and touched the roll of cash. She kept digging and she pulled out three more coffee cans from beneath the rubble and each one held a roll of cash of various size. A savings hidden away and then forgotten and then remembered again in the swirling winds of her mind. She dropped the rolls of money into the grocery sack with the random gathering. Ran her fingers across her pallid face. Her eyes like deepset windows into a sprawling world. She seemed to gather herself and she let out a great exhale as if arriving at a moment of resignation.

She stood and straightened her housecoat. Stepped out of her slippers and brushed off her ashy feet and then she stepped back into them and she tucked the grocery sack under her arm and she made for the front door. She opened it and the nightwind greeted her and she gazed out into the darkness. A traveler readied for some journey.

A starblown sky above the winding road that led from the house. The road badly patched and bumpy and she stumbled twice but caught herself both times. Cursing the uneven ground in quick insults before returning again to the harried conversations of her lost world. She wandered from the road and into a field where she pushed through the kneehigh grass. Where searching eyes busied with the hunt stopped and stared in the direction of her shuffling and the wind pushed at her wild hair and slushed through the wild grass and on the other side of the field she entered into the woods where the moonglow gave shadows through the trees and where she held out her hands and touched the trunks as she moved through the forest. The dark guardians willing to give her pass. The wind shook leaves from the limbs and they fell around her in swirls of decay as she stepped across the leafstrewn earth. The small crunches of aged and careful steps.

She was not afraid until she was deep into the woods. She stopped and looked around and whatever confused purpose had been there to guide her slipped off into the dark and left her alone. There was wind and there were the calls of the night and between the black treelimbs there were stars and moon. The heavens infinite. She leaned her back against a tree and hugged herself as if suddenly cold and she began to cry.

She cried and began walking again in no direction. Moving through the woods in a confused and careful gait and beginning to call out the names of people who passed through her mind. Names that both meant something and meant nothing. Her father and a woman she once sat next to on an airplane and a pigtailed friend from childhood and the old man who taught her to ride a horse and the boy who sacked her groceries once upon a time. The wind gained strength and the limbs swayed and bent and her hair whipped on her head and she clutched the sack with both hands and called out to anyone who might be listening and she lost a slipper and moved with one bare foot and panicked eyes and a deepening fear that something in the dark was going to devour her. She was lost in head and heart and soul and she stopped and stared up at the moon and she began to question it as if it had the answers to the universe. Who are you and where am I and what are we and the questions continued and carried her as she meandered through the dark. Walking into branches that scratched her face and bits of leaf and limb getting stuck in her hair and she lost her other slipper and she was no longer crying and no longer questioning the moon but now transformed into something ancient and mindless and driven by some preordained task as if she was no longer of grayed flesh and bone but instead a shapeless spirit of the wood that drifted timelessly. She moved through the night in the random pattern of wind and then through the trees she saw the firelight. She fixed her eyes on the flames as she pushed away lowhanging limbs and crunched across the leaves and her mouth moved as if speaking but she was soundless as she came into the clearing.

Two crouching silhouettes next to the fire. Two figures rising when they looked up at the old woman who emerged from the wood. Twigs in her hair and a torn housecoat and bare feet and sticklike legs and the distant gaze. She regarded the dark figures and then she looked again into the starstruck night. At the marblewhite moon. She let her arms fall to her sides in a great release and she spoke in some language they did not understand. She then fell silent and the sack dropped from her hand and spilled onto the ground. A spindle of cash rolled forward and settled in the firelight and there was no judgment among them but for the emptiness in which they all stood.

2

They left the dying fire and walked out of the clearing, the tawny light on their backs and darkness before them. Their car parked on the roadside. A big four-door thing, long as a boat. Two hubcaps missing. The antenna snapped off. Each man lit a cigarette before climbing in and closing doors and then they sat there smoking and staring through the bugsmeared windshield. Something small and brighteyed crossed the road. It stopped and looked at the car and then continued on its journey and disappeared into the brush. Falling leaves swirled in the wind and fell in the moonshine like flakes of rust.

One man sniffed and the other coughed as the car filled with smoke. The driver rolled down the window. He smoked and scratched at his beard before flicking out the cigarette, a little red spray as the butt bounced on the road. The man in the passenger seat smoked more methodically and was still at it when the car cranked and the headlights split the dark. The big car moved in a great lurch and began its descent from the hillside, filling the night with a low rumble.

They drove through the darkness. Past rolling pastures lined by leaning fenceposts held erect by strands of barbed wire. Past gatherings of hardwoods and over skinny bridges with rotted rails where the moon reflected in the wobbled creekwater. The big car cruised around the bends in the road where deer stood backed away and still and waiting and it rolled through desolate four-way stops where there was nothing and no one and they drove on with their redtipped cigarettes across the fallen landscape of the autumn where the fields had turned the color of sand and the stars stabbed the sky in darts of silver.

Neither man spoke.

They emerged from the unmarked country roads and turned onto a two-lane highway. Mailboxes stood on the roadside at the end of gravel driveways and sleeping houses sat quiet and peaceful back in the gloom. Dogs slept on porches and raised their heads to regard the loud thing moving through the night and then returned to slumber as the growl of the engine disappeared. The lights of the world appeared in the fluorescents of gas stations and in flashing red signals and in yellowed street lamps and then disappeared in the rearview mirror as the car followed the highway right through the meager town and entered a new dark.

Thirteen more miles of silence between them and pine trees and the rise and dip of the hills and then as if leaving one country and crossing into another the landscape bottomed out. The car now traveled a flat terrain in a rhythmic glide as if trolling across the serenity of lakewater. Spanish moss hung from treelimbs in gray and gathered clumps and the long and drooping limbs of the willows swayed in the wind and the swamp slurped up against the roadside as if only waiting for the command from some weather god to swallow what was left of the raised earth.

The frame that held the child's drawing of the angel sat between them on the benchseat. The man in the passenger seat picked it up. Flicked his cigarette lighter and looked at it in the solitary light of the flame. He ran his thumb across an angel wing and then he set the frame back on the seat and gazed out into the night. The driver looked over at him and wanted to ask why he had bothered to bring it along but he only gave a silent look of disgust and his eyes returned to the road.

And then there it was. The allnight truckstop sat in isolation as if it had long ago been misplaced and forgotten. The car bumped across the potholed parking lot and stopped in front of the glass doors of the diner. A handful of cats hunted around a dumpster. Two eighteen-wheelers parked off behind the gas pumps. Darkness closed all around as if this place had been created as a sojourn before some final plummet. The neon sign read OPEN in the front window and bugs danced around in the cottoncandy glow. From behind bent and twisted blinds the lights of the diner cut into the night in awkward slants. The two men sat there and stared until the man in the passenger seat coughed and shifted in his seat.

"Well. Ain't you gonna say something?"

The driver grabbed his cigarette pack from the dashboard.

"About what?"

The driver then looked at himself in the rearview mirror

and rubbed at his bloodshot eyes before climbing out of the car. The passenger watched as the bearded man pulled open the door to the diner and disappeared inside.

"About what," he muttered.

He then got out and followed.

3

They sat in a booth against the window. An ashtray between them. Above them a ceiling fan turned slowly and the knocking of kitchen work came from behind a swinging door. A tiredlooking woman with her sleeves rolled above her elbows brought them cups of coffee and then she asked if she could bum a cigarette. The man with the beard held his pack to her and she took one and then she pulled a lighter from her apron pocket and lit the cigarette and said I hope you like breakfast because that's all we got.

The men nodded. She shuffled away and sat down on a stool at the end of the counter. At the other end of the counter a man in a flannel shirt read a ragged paperback and sipped a beer. The men watched and waited for her to pass the breakfast order on to someone somewhere but she only sat and smoked.

Burdean was the older of the two by nearly twenty years. His beard had begun the transformation from coffeebrown to gray and his eyes wore the lines of an outlier. The skin of his hands and face was fatigued by decades of cigarette smoke and the strike of the sun in the days when he worked on a roofing crew or a construction crew or whatever crew he could find to take him for a few weeks until he had what he thought was enough cash in his pocket to quit and survive for a while. Until he decided that it was too goddamn hot or too goddamn cold or just too goddamn pretty outside to be wasting his time working on any of those crews and the list of things he would do for money grew longer. And those were the things that should be done in the dark. He lifted his cup and sipped and looked at the man who was sharing this strange night with him. His washed-blue eyes and the flips in his hair and the fading expression of boyhood still clinging to the edges of the hard world.

"You might as well stop thinking about it," Burdean said.

"I don't see how you could say such a thing," Keal said.

"There ain't no room for conscience in what we're doing."

"We didn't do what we're doing. We did something else."

"Just the same."

The waitress got up from the counter and slipped behind the swinging door. Keal stabbed out his cigarette and then bent down the blinds and looked outside.

"What are you looking for?"

"I don't know. Nothing."

He removed his fingers and the blinds slapped back in place. In the kitchen the waitress argued with someone and then there was the clatter of pots and pans and then silence. She returned to the end of the counter and sat picking the polish from her fingernails.

Keal could not be still. He adjusted in his seat. Bumped his knuckles on the table. Rubbed at the stubble on his face. Scratched his ear. Flicked the cigarette lighter. Counted the sugar packets. Bumped his knuckles on the table again.

"You got to quit it," Burdean said.

"Quit what?"

"Squirming around like you're waiting on the verdict."

"That's a funny way to put it."

"I ain't trying to be funny. I'm trying to get you to settle down or you need to go sit somewhere else."

"Where you want me to go sit?"

"Anyfuckingwhere."

A bell dinged. The waitress got up from the counter and pushed through the swinging door and then returned carrying two plates covered in bacon and eggs and grits. She set the plates down in front of them and then she refilled their coffee. The diner door opened and a man in a cowboy hat whistled at her. The waitress grinned and then she returned the coffeepot to the warmer and she followed the cowboy out into the parking lot.

"What are we doing here?" Keal asked.

"This is where we're supposed to deliver and I thought maybe there would be somebody sitting around who looks like they could give us a clue as to why there is a light inside that church."

"Are we going back out there?" Keal said.

"Not tonight."

"How come?"

"They wanted it done before daybreak."

"There's time."

"Maybe."

"I wish you'd tell me what we're supposed to be looking for."

"I told you already. You got the same information I got. The way it was explained to me is to go around the back of the church house and some doors open and go down into a cellar. Whatever it is we'll know it when we see it."

"That don't make no sense."

"It don't make no sense why there was a light on inside that abandoned old place either. But it was."

"We should go back and see if it's dark inside again."

"I was getting ready to when the ghost came out of the woods."

"She wasn't a ghost."

"She will be before long. If she ain't already fell down a hole."

"I still say we should go back."

"Hush and eat."

Burdean picked up his fork and mixed the eggs and grits together. Keal only stared at his food.

He had been plagued by dreams beginning in childhood. Seeing things in his sleep before they happened. A foul ball cracking a windshield at the baseball game. The stumble of the blondheaded gym teacher as she strode across the playground. The leering eyes of the man behind the counter at the gas station as he gave his mother her change. Small moments in the mundane motion of the everyday that he recognized the instant they occurred. Moments he found contentment in when he was able to connect the premonitions to reality and he began to believe that he was in possession of a special gift.

That he was privy to some secret. As he grew into a teenager the moments began to occur more often and he believed he could anticipate them. His eyes alive to the movements and colors of the world as if studying fish in a fishbowl. Knowing what someone was going to say before they said it. Seeing what girls were sitting on the tailgate at the river before pulling up beside them. Hearing his mother's voice before she spoke. An anticipation living inside him as he remained on the watch for the next thing and then feeling a pronounced satisfaction when it appeared.

Then the dreams changed.

The figures grew unrecognizable. Dusky and vague and moving about in shifts of gray. And the landscapes were no longer the places he knew. The trailer he and his mother shared and the pond behind it. The pool hall that let the high school kids come in and sometimes sold them beer. Classrooms and hallways. The deep greens of the backroads in the long light of summer days. The settings of his dreams became alleyways. Empty buildings. Sprawling wastelands of dust and smoke. The clouds rolled like boulders and the wind pushed the black trees and the figures were nameless and faceless and shrouded in shadow and scared the hell out of him and he would wake in the middle of the night with his arms outstretched and shoving at the dark. He did not know why the temper of the dreams had changed or where they came from and his demeanor transformed in the waking hours as he began to fear the creatures of his sleep. Believing that someone or something had emerged from the nightmares and was only waiting for him to walk around the wrong corner at the wrong time and then snatch him into the void.

It was then that the mold appeared and returned his dreams to some notion of reality. And it was the same dream again and again. A bright and cloudless afternoon. He returned from school in his pickup. His mother was at work. He walked across the yard and as he climbed the concrete steps and reached for the trailer door he noticed the specks of purple and green growing around the door frame. Each night and each dream the mold spread a little further. Stretching out from the frame and growing around the windows and reaching toward the roof and as the mold spread he walked slower and slower from his pickup to the trailer. Afraid to reach the door. Afraid to open the door. Believing it had crept inside and not wanting to see it or breathe it and then as the mold covered the entirety of the trailer in the colors of a bruise and as he finally found the courage to open the door the moment was interrupted as he heard the sound of his mother's car and he looked up to see her coming along the dirt driveway and she waved to him from her open window as she parked and got out and walked toward him and he began to yell at her to get back. Don't come any further. Stay away just stay away but she ignored him and walked right past him and she opened the door and went inside and closed it behind her.

It was the next day that she had sat with him at the kitchen table and explained that she was sick and that it wasn't going to last long. He only held her hands and looked into her sinking eyes and said I know. I know. She didn't ask him how he knew. They only sat together in the quiet.

Burdean took his last bite and then he pointed at Keal's plate. "Aren't you gonna eat?"

Keal picked up a piece of bacon and bit off the end. The diner door opened and the waitress returned and Burdean lifted his coffee cup and waved it at her. Then he slid from the booth and he took off his coat and laid it over the back of the seat. The waitress came over with the coffeepot and gave them a refill. Burdean asked her where the bathroom was and she pointed at a hallway at the end of the counter and told him to go that way and keep walking.

Keal had turned eighteen the week before he buried her. The sickness had spread quickly and he did what he could to help but when she died she was only a shriveled suggestion of the woman she had been. The woman who worked two and sometimes three jobs and threw the football with him in the yard and took him swimming at the springfed creek where the water was teethchattering cold. She had been lean and strong and she kept in motion and she tanned easily and she taught him to drive a stickshift. The woman he buried was not that. Grayrimmed eyes and sallow cheeks. On the night after she was lowered into the grave he dreamed of a mold that spread across the earth and poisoned the young and the old and it blackened the wildflowers and the kudzu and he woke with a scream and once he gathered himself in the dark and remembered where he was and what had happened and that he was alone in this world he swore to himself in that rattled moment that he would never sleep again.

He tried.

At first he trained himself to go for days with only sporadic napping of thirty or fortyfive minutes. Then he trained himself to go for weeks in the same way. Only sometimes spending a few hours in slumber. There was no way to stop dreaming but the lack of sleep kept him anxious and quicktempered one instant and deadeyed and sluggish the next and he didn't have the focus to make connections. His life became something of a dream itself. Two sentences behind in conversations. Mindlessly running red lights. Picking up the phone and ordering food and then forgetting where he had ordered it from as he drove toward town. When he experienced something of a premonition he only rubbed at his eyes and then left the room or the bar or wherever he was before the scene played itself out, avoiding the confirmation of what he knew was coming.

And then it would finally hit him, a blanket of exhaustion wrapping him and pulling him into extended periods of deadened sleep. Nineteen hours at a time. Twentyfour hours. Twentyeight hours. He would wake to angry messages from bosses and angry messages from women and he was years into the sleepless experiment when he couldn't take it anymore and he decided that it had all been a fabrication. None of it was real. He had been a boy with a terrific imagination and then a teenager with a terrific imagination and then a young man with a terrific imagination and each version of himself was full of more shit than the one before. He told himself over and over that there was no such thing as seeing things before they happen and there was no such thing as a bridge between what you dream and what is to come and with all the declaring and all the self-condemnation the dreams stopped. He discovered that when you do not care about the world there is nothing left to unravel.

Burdean returned from the bathroom and plopped down in the booth. He stared at Keal's plate still covered with eggs and grits and then he tapped out a cigarette and held it between his fingers.

"If it'll make you feel better you can give me your half," Burdean said.

"What?"

"Your two rolls of cash. Blood money you can wash clean as the driven snow. All you need to do is hand it over and that old woman will slip off to wherever your mind needs her to slip off."

"I ain't worried about that old woman no more."

"Then quit looking like it."

Like some hibernating malady it had returned. Keal was now sleeping only two or three hours at a time. The dream-world had changed, with the reoccurring image of a dark and shifting figure moving with no features or form. The only thing he gathered about the figure was that it was a woman who was lost and searching for something. Something that not even she could understand. He had tried not to think about the dream but it held the same strength as the dream of the cancerous mold that came for his mother and though it had been seventeen years since she had died, when he looked up from the fire and the old woman lurched from the woods he was arrowstruck with the feeling that it was his mother returning to this world in her weak and wraithlike form to say something to him. To give him an instruction or warning or to deliver some insight into the mysteries of the beyond. He had been both stupefied and expectant of her appearance but instead of engaging her as if she was either his mother or some embodiment of her spirit he only stood speechless alongside Burdean as he had taken the old woman's money.

Keal still pictured Burdean gently gathering the rolls of cash and then the woman kneeling to try to recover the contents of the grocery sack spilled across the ground and her mouth moved in mindless babbling and Keal just watching as Burdean moved around her, looking down at her and his shadow falling across her bony frame until he pulled out his knife and unfolded the blade. And when he reached for the old woman Keal came alive and screamed for Burdean to stop and the sudden sound caused them both to look up at Keal who was moving toward them with his arm reaching for the visitor from the darkness. Burdean paused with the blade pointed at the back of the woman's head and Keal reached down and slipped his hands under her arms and lifted her to her feet. He tried to talk to her. Tried to find out where she came from or what her name was or what the living hell she was doing out in the middle of the night but her eyes looked everywhere but at him and she spoke in pieces of sentences that had no relation to his questions and Burdean told him to get the hell out of the way. I've seen people act crazier than this and then five minutes later they will tell the law clear as day who you are and what they saw you do.

Keal waved away the knife and shook his head at Burdean. Burdean held still as if only waiting for Keal to get clear but Keal took the old woman by the hands and moved her away from Burdean and said I'll walk her back into the woods if you'll put that damn thing away. She don't know the difference between up and down and she sure as shit won't remember me and you. Burdean folded the blade and tucked it into his pocket. Keal took the old woman by the hand and said I'll take you home. Come on with me. Her fingers like sticks. Her bare feet dirty and scratched. Wild eyes dancing in the firelight.

When he moved she moved with him. They stepped away from the fire and eased toward the treeline where the light died away and just as they entered the woods Burdean called out. This will haunt you. His voice like some reckoning in the darkness. Keal looked back over his shoulder at the black figure who stood smoking and staring and the image of his own mother disappearing inside the diseased trailer passed into his mind and seized him. This will haunt you. The words soaking through him. The old woman was trying to pull away from him now and her movement returned him to this night and to her journey back to wherever she had come from and he walked with her into the depths of the darkwood until she was talking no more but only humming to herself and he let go of her hand and set her adrift back into the dark.

Burdean lit his cigarette. Keal pushed away the plate and said you can have the rest if you want it. Keal then took a sip of coffee and felt the two rolls of cash in his coat pocket. His half of the unexpected booty. Burdean smacked his lips and would not stop frowning at him and Keal peeked between the blinds again and looked into the parking lot and he imagined the wild-haired woman wandering through the moonstruck night and he imagined the spirits stalking her and he heard her frightened whimpers. He let go of the blinds and he got up from the booth.

"I'm going to the can," he said.

He walked to the end of the counter and down the hallway and toward the bathroom. At the end of the hallway there was another door and he opened it and it led outside.

On a concrete square surrounded by garbage cans there was a skinny young man sitting in a folding chair, wearing a cook's apron and holding a joint in one hand and a beer in the other. He stared at the space between his feet and he never looked up as Keal stepped past him and snuck around the backside of the diner. When the engine of the big car cranked and the head-lights lit the diner Burdean didn't bother to get up. He only finished his cigarette and then finished Keal's plate of eggs and grits and then he wiped his mouth and walked to the pay phone that hung in the hallway. He dropped a quarter in and dialed and when the voice on the other end answered it said this better be damn good for you to be calling me this time of night.

"Mind your tone," Burdean said. "And get your ass up and come and get me."

4

She wandered as burdenless as a child. The world not bleak and shadowed but simply the place of being. No need for understanding or reason as she traversed the night in delicate steps as if she were not alone and vulnerable but only crossing through the wooded hills of tolerance and immune to the complexities of time.

She stopped and stared up at the universe through a break in the trees. Small whispers came from her mouth in the clouded breaths of a cool night.

A voice echoed through the woods.

Hey. Hey.

But she was deaf to anything but the voices inside her head.

She did not know she was being observed. She did not know she was being followed. She was unaware of how hunting creatures could move silently through the dark and stalking hours.

5

Keal drove the big car back through the swampland and
then it rose up and over the hills and around the bends
and drifted through the open spaces of field and sky,
ambling through the dark and searching for the clearing where
they had built the fire. Where the old woman had appeared and
then disappeared.

It all looked the same to Keal. He stopped twice when he
believed he had found the spot but there were no remnants of a
fire and he drove on. The window rolled down now, trying to
smell smoke. Trying to listen for any sound in the night.

He was moments from giving up and returning to Burdean
to face the music when he noticed the depressions of tire tracks
in the soft ground of the roadside. He stopped. Got out of the car
and looked at the tracks in the red glow of the taillights and he
recognized the ascension in the road. He hopped back in the car
and eased along and in fifty yards he came to the clearing.

He killed the big car and it died with a cough. He picked up the framed drawing of the angel from the benchseat and he held it in the soft light of the dashboard and he imagined the tiny hand drawing the heavenly thing. The child's imagination at work. The vision of glory sprung from what he could only hope had been innocence.

He set the frame down and got out. He stepped across a ditch and walked over to the ash and embers of the fire. He then crossed the clearing and stepped into the woods and began calling out for the old woman. Not knowing a name but only calling out into the unknown.

Hey. Hey.

Getting a little louder each time. Hearing his calls echo and then drop off into the dark. He tried to remember the direction that he had guided her and then set her free to go and the notion of trusting her to return to anywhere or anything struck him with the gutpunch of absurdity. His pace quickened. The pulse of wandering. His calls more frequent.

He came to a stream and he stopped. The silvery glide of moonwashed water across the rocks and clumps of leaves. He then closed his eyes and tried to disappear into the images of his dreams. Searching the subconscious for the direction to the woman. Trying to conjure his power of prediction. He remained still and tried to bury himself deep within but there was no superpower to conjure as it would not come in the waking hours.

When finally he gave up and gazed again into the woods he did not find the woman but instead he found a pair of bluewhite eyes staring at him. Bluewhite eyes caught in the moonlight. Bluewhite eyes as still as a mountain as if they had always been there waiting for him to cross the years and bear witness.

He stepped across the stream. The eyes did not move. He reached down and picked up a fallen limb and held it like a club and he felt the rot and knew it was useless but it somehow made sense to be holding something.

He moved several slow steps and a nightbird sang and the eyes upon him were patient. Keal envied the predator. The ability to stare and gauge with nothing more than survival as an impetus. No other train of thought more complex than this is what I want. He thought of the pistol beneath the benchseat in the car and he thought of the tire iron in the trunk and then he wondered if the eyes were standing over the old woman and if there was blood dripping from the fangs beneath the eyes and if she would be one meal or two or three and he squeezed the rotted limb and his fingers sunk into the sodden wood just as the eyes shifted and the wolf turned its head to the side as if to judge their isolation. The moonlight brushed the thick coat of the predator and a length of black lay at its feet and Keal wondered if she had even had the capacity to scream when she was taken down.

Keal listened for a whimper. For any pain.

The eyes turned back to him. He would not run now with the image of the old woman there against the cold earth with her throat opened by the wolf.

He called out again but this time when the word came out of his mouth it was not what he had been expecting to say.

Raylene.

When he heard his mother's name empty into the dark it was as if it had been spoken by a visitor there beside him who had no fear of reaching into another world.

He called again. Raylene.

The wolf shifted. Backed away from whatever it was standing over.

Raylene.

Keal knelt and felt around for something to throw at it but there was no need as the wolf continued to back away. The bluewhite eyes in slow retreat as if to offer some pardon to the intruder into its territory. Keal stayed down on one knee and watched until the wolf turned its head around and walked off into the night and when Keal rose to his feet and began walking toward the fallen prey he noticed that the wolf would move a few feet and then stop and look back at him. Move again and then stop and look back at him. As if to say, if you want to find what you are looking for then follow me. Keal continued toward the fallen black figure but kept his eyes on the wolf and when he was finally close enough to see what he was afraid to see he saw instead a young deer motionless and torn where the wolf had been standing. A great wash of relief came over him and he said his mother's name again with the hard breath of exhaust. The deer was only in the beginnings of butcher and Keal looked to the wolf again as if to deliver some type of gratitude. The wolf looked back at him. Waited.

Keal dropped the rotted limb and he walked in the direction of the wolf who had begun to lead Keal across its terrain. Man and animal together in some strange understanding. The wolf moved on and continued to check over its shoulder for its follower and Keal wanted to call out again for the woman but believed his voice would disrupt the wolf and so he only followed and listened and gave up trying to make sense of anything that was happening.

The wolf and Keal both froze when the shotguns sounded.

Gunshots in hard succession that rolled across the night and then all fell silent once again.

The wolf glanced back at Keal and Keal looked toward the sound of the blasts. Realized the disruption came from the direction of the old church that he and Burdean had gone looking for and then retreated from when they unexpectedly saw the wobbly light shining from behind the old arched windows.

One more blast. And then a howl.

When all settled in the dark, the wolf resumed its crossing and began to trot through the woods. Keal trotted behind it. There was nothing to do but go and see.

6

Burdean was pacing and smoking outside the café when the truck rolled into the gravel lot. The truck wore a homemade paint job of camouflage, covered in splotches of green and black.

When the truck stopped Burdean opened the door. The inside reeked of numerous cluttered scents and Burdean had to shove three empty tallboy cans from the seat and onto the floorboard before he climbed in.

"It's about damn time," Burdean said as he shut the door.

"I'd prefer if you don't smoke up in here."

Burdean took a long drag and then blew the smoke toward the man.

"If you're not vomiting already from the same things I'm smelling in this truck cab then my cigarette sure as hell ain't gonna kill you. Consider it an air freshener."

The man shook his head and took his foot off the brake and

the truck shifted across the gravel. Burdean pointed back down the highway and said go that way.

"There ain't nothing that way," the man answered.

"You got enough gas?" Burdean said. "Gauge says empty."

"It's broke."

"Course it is."

"You still ain't told me where we're going," the man said.

"I just did. That way. And that's all I'm gonna say about it until I point us all the way there."

"All the way where?"

"Shut your mouth. Drive."

Burdean was quickly reminded why he had taken on Keal. Because of dumb shit like this. Ed was the kind of man who moved through life blanketed by his own indifference. He had no woman and had never had one for more than a minute and his beard was that of a wolfman and covered damn near his entire face and if it didn't involve a bar stool or a deer stand or a recliner he was little interested. Burdean had never seen him wear anything but one of three flannel shirts and at times he seemed like some relic that had always been right in the spot he was in. All of which made him perfectly suitable for whatever Burdean asked him to do. But the man was incapable of silence.

"I was sleeping you know," Ed said.

"Most of the world is."

"Well. Here anyway. Not in Europe."

The truck passed across the lowlands. Burdean finished his cigarette and stuck the butt into an empty beer can and then he lit another and he raised his hand to Ed to shut him up before he even said it. But he said it anyway.

"You know I don't like cigarettes, Burdean."

"I'm aware."

"I'm just saying."

"You know the caution light up here in a few miles?"

"Yeah."

"Go left when you get there."

"Then what," Ed said.

"Then keep driving."

"How far we going?"

"You sure you got gas?"

Ed shrugged.

"Let me tell you something, Ed. You're my friend. We've done a lot of shit together. But if this truck runs out of gas I'm gonna bury your ass wherever it rolls to a stop and you damn well know I mean it."

Ed was quiet until the caution light. He turned left and in a few miles the truck rose into the hills.

"I mean, I'm pretty sure I got gas."

Burdean finished and lit another cigarette. Then he reached into his pocket and pulled out one of the rolls of cash he had taken from the old woman. He stripped the rubber band and counted out five twenty-dollar bills and showed them to Ed.

"This is a hundred bucks. It's yours unless you say another word. For every word you say from now until the time I tell you to stop the truck and let me out I'm gonna take away twenty dollars. You got it?"

"Yep."

Burdean took away a twenty.

Ed rolled his head around on his thick neck and shifted in his seat as if struck by a sudden and sore discomfort.

"What was that? I couldn't hear you," Burdean said.

Ed glanced at the remaining bills and wrenched the steering wheel and drove on.

When Burdean saw the big car in the headlights in the same spot where he and Keal had parked hours before, he pointed and said right there. Ed stopped the truck in the middle of the road. Burdean got out and stood in the open doorway and looked around.

Ed raised his hand.

"You can talk now," Burdean said. He handed him the eighty dollars.

"You need me to stay?"

"Maybe. Hold on."

"Cause I can stay."

"I heard you."

Burdean closed the truck door. Walked around and passed through the headlight beams. He then leaned and looked inside the big car and the keys dangled from the ignition. He raised and told Ed he could leave.

Ed rolled down the window and said what the hell you doing out here anyway.

Burdean didn't answer. He stood with his hands on his hips. He knew Keal was wandering through the woods searching for that old woman and he didn't want to go and look for him.

"Nothing. I ain't doing nothing but sitting right here waiting."

"On what?"

"Go on. I already told you."

The shotgun blasts could not be missed. Both turned their heads simultaneously in the direction of the booms.

"Maybe I'll go," Ed said.

Burdean reached into his coat and pulled out the roll and peeled off five more twenties.

"Maybe I need you to stay," Burdean said.

Ed took the money through the open window. Burdean turned and opened the car door and he took the keys from the ignition and then he reached beneath the seat and pulled out a pistol. He tucked it in his pants and then he walked to the front of the truck.

Another boom rose and fell and sunk into the dead of night.

7

The church sat back from the road and in the day it would fall into the shadows of the farreaching limbs of red maples and white oaks. A simple and strong sanctuary, built a century and a half earlier by ordinary hill folk. The church framed and floored with planks from the same hardwoods of the land surrounding it. A set of arched windows above the front door. Windows lining each side to give sunlight to the pews and pulpit.

The church had doubled as a schoolhouse in its earliest days and there was a cellar beneath that served as a storm shelter where over the decades nervous and prayerful neighbors had sat together in the amber glow of kerosene lamps and listened to the pounding of the rain or the howls of tornados. Flaking paint fell like snowflakes in a hard wind and moss grew on the roof and birds nested in the crux of the steeple. A small and abandoned cemetery with blackened and cracked headstones lay nestled in the woods to the side of the church. Wisteria vines hung from the treelimbs and brushed across the graves. With each passing year the sag of time and gravity drew the neglected house of worship closer to the ground.

Keal and Burdean had been told to go to the church and go into the cellar. For what, Burdean had asked. You'll know it when you see it, he was told. When you have it call back and I will tell you what to do.

Keal got there first, following the wolf through the woods and then when the wolf saw the gathering of headlights around the church it darted off into the night. Keal stood behind a tree trunk and watched the scene.

One vehicle sat silent and dark parked by the roadside. A van and a truck were parked beside the church with their engines running and headlights illuminating the decaying structure. The side door of the van was open. A body lay half in and half out of the side door. Another body lay beneath the grille of the truck. The windshield whitened with gunshot. Two more bodies were folded across one another in a pose of morbid copulation on the ground beside the cellar doors and the doors to the cellar were open wide.

Keal listened to the stillrunning engines of the vehicles. Listened for voices. Waited for movement. The exhaust from the tailpipes formed a haze that drifted across the churchyard and transfixed the moment in the miasma of an illusion.

Nothing.

Then headlights appeared along the road. Moving hesitantly toward the church and the carnage. Keal slipped from behind the tree and moved closer and hid behind another tree. The approaching vehicle was a truck and it stopped on the roadside next to the parked car. Keal stared at it and everyone and everything held still in a long moment of caution. In the east the faintest light of a spinning world began to transform the horizon from black to blue.

Burdean got out of the truck. He left the door open and when he passed in the headlights Keal saw he was holding a pistol at his side. As he moved closer to the church Burdean raised the pistol and held it at the ready and he looked into the open door of the van. Poked the lifeless body with his foot. Then he turned and moved past the body sprawled in front of the truck and he checked the truck cab and there was no one else and he was beginning to move toward the cellar when Keal stepped out from behind the tree and crossed the graveyard and when Burdean heard the movement of his footsteps he turned and aimed and almost shot the shadowy man stepping around a headstone with his hands raised in submission.

"Don't," Keal said.

He kept coming until he was in the lights. Burdean lowered the pistol and shook his head but then he raised his finger to his mouth to shush Keal from saying anything more. He then waved him over. When Keal crossed between the vehicles Burdean pointed to the ground and Keal knelt and picked up a sawed-off shotgun that lay next to the body in front of the truck. He then joined Burdean and they stood beside the fold of the dead beside the cellar doors and stared down the steps. The hard call of silence coming from the black beneath.

Burdean reached into his coat pocket and pulled out a small flashlight. He clicked it on, the beam the size of a silver dollar. He shined the meager light down into the dark and they descended.

The brick steps were crumbling. Tiny nests and tiny skeletons tucked into the corners of the stairs. A dozen steps down and when they reached the bottom there was another man. Facedown. A bloodstained back. A set of keys lay next to his open hand on the grimy and leafstrewn floor.

Burdean raised the flashlight and pointed it into a dark so absolute that the light seemed to suck away into nothing. But they eased forward. Guns raised. The cellar long and narrow and they stepped over two more bodies that had been there for more than this night and the smell of decay was profound and eye-watering but they kept on and then Keal grabbed Burdean's arm and stopped him. Keal motioned ahead and Burdean turned off the flashlight. At the other end of the cellar a strip of muted light came from beneath what had to be a door.

They waited and listened in the black world.

Burdean clicked the flashlight back on. He ran the beam across the floor and there was nothing and no one left between them and the door.

The men walked softly. Slowly. When they reached the door they paused. Burdean leaned his ear against it. Raised his head and then nodded to Keal to open it. Burdean took a step back and raised the pistol and the flashlight together and then he nodded again and Keal turned the handle and yanked open the door.

The room was small and draped in cobwebs. Oblong faces with Xs for eyes and animal figures with mismatched heads and bodies had been spraypainted on the moldy brick walls. There was a cross chiseled into the brick and a chalky stick figure drawn beneath it with its arms extended as if hoisting the cross and carrying the weight. An oil lamp in the corner gave dull yellowbrown light. The old woman looked at them with little surprise as if expecting their arrival. She was still holding her sack of possessions. Still cut and scratched from traipsing through the woods. Still losteyed. But she was as soundless as a breeze as she stared back at them.

Standing next to her was a little girl.

8

K eal took the old woman by the hand and the old woman took the little girl by the hand and Burdean walked before them and shined the light and they navigated the bodies and the cellar dark and moved up the stairs and back out into the falling night. When they rose out of the cellar Burdean told Keal to take them to the truck and don't listen to a damn word the guy driving says, just put them in the truck with him and then come back over here.

When the girl and the woman were in the truck with Ed, Keal and Burdean stood between the headlights. Both men smoked. Both men with their hands on their hips. Both men in a state of speechlessness over where they were and what they'd found. Keal was the first to break the silence just as the first stars began to disappear in the draw of dawn.

"I ain't doing this shit," he said.

"What shit?"

"You might as well stop it, Burdean. I ain't doing this shit."

"Stop what? What shit are you talking about? Because if you know I'd be happy if you told me."

"I ain't being part of taking that little girl nowhere."

Burdean smoked. Paced.

"We don't even know that's what we were supposed to find," he said.

"Like hell, Burdean. There's a good goshdamn reason you weren't told what we were after and that's pretty much it. I ain't taking her nowhere and neither are you."

"We got to take her somewhere. We can't leave her in this hillbilly morgue."

"That ain't what I meant."

"Just hush a minute."

Burdean tossed his cigarette and moved from one dead body to the next. Pushing them over and seeing if he recognized faces or scars or tattoos or anything. He didn't. Then he looked into the truck cab and he looked into the van and there was not one thing he could make sense out of from any of it. There was nothing else to take. He returned to Keal.

"I know that old woman has given you some kind of holy awakening but we got to get rid of her first," Burdean said. "She's got to live around here close."

"We gonna just set her off down the road?"

"Somebody will find her."

"What if they don't?"

"It ain't my problem, Keal. It ain't your problem either whether you know it or not."

The truck horn honked. The men looked at Ed who was waving out of the window.

Burdean and Keal walked to the road.

"What?" Burdean said.

"She won't shut up," Ed said.

"Who?"

The old woman was shaking her finger and talking about the turkey she needed to get out of the oven. The little girl sat quietly between them on the benchseat.

Keal walked around to her side and opened the door.

"We'll get the turkey out of the oven if you can tell us where you live."

"I ain't got time. I ain't got time for all that. Damn turkey is gonna burn up."

"We can get it. Just tell us where you live."

"I can hear Maureen fussing about it already. She can't never stop complaining when something ain't right."

"I told you," Ed said.

The old woman held her sack on her lap. Keal asked if he could look in it and she squeezed it to her chest. But when he said please and he held his hands out with his palms up as if readying to catch her fall, she relented. Keal looked through the contents and in the jumble of possessions he found an empty envelope with a postmark that was over a year old. The name on the envelope read Wanetah Wilkins.

"Are you Wanetah?"

She didn't answer. Or couldn't answer. Keal then read the address.

"I remember passing this road when I was trying to get back over here."

"We got to get the hell away from this place," Burdean said. And then he told Ed to get out from behind the wheel and climb in the back.

"It's cold, Burdean."

"Get your ass out and get back there or give me my damn money back."

Ed got out and climbed in the truck bed. Burdean sat behind the wheel and slammed the door and he told Keal to get in.

DAYBREAK

9

They found the road and what they hoped was the old woman's house in the smokeblue break of day. Burdean stopped at the edge of the driveway and Keal saw Wanetah Wilkins on the wad of mail shoved into the mailbox. He then helped her out of the truck, coaxing her with promises of getting the turkey out of the oven on time.

"What turkey?" she said.

"Don't touch nothing in there," Burdean said.

He led her across the dewsoaked grass and to the front door that she had left open. He walked her inside and was surprised and not surprised by the hoarding. The old woman plopped down onto a wad of clothes that were piled in the seat of a recliner as her exhaustion overcame her confusion. Keal followed the trail between the clutter that led to the kitchen. The table was covered in empty cereal boxes and piles of mail and dirty coffee cups and he pushed the mess around in hopes of finding some name or some clue as to who he may call to help her but it made no more sense to him than it did to her.

He then heard a snore. He looked through the doorway and she had stretched her body out across the pile of clothes and her head was back and her mouth wide open.

A dishrag was draped over the sink faucet and he picked it up. He wrapped it around his hand and was reaching for the telephone that he expected to have no connection when it rang. He stopped. As he listened to it ring he was interrupted by Burdean coming through the front door. Keal left the kitchen and met Burdean at the recliner where the old woman slept.

"Let me tell you something," Burdean said. "That truck out there is leaving."

The phone kept ringing. Keal looked toward the kitchen.

"Don't even think about it," Burdean said and he turned around and walked out. Keal hesitated. Took one more look at the old woman. The wrinkled skin. The frailty of her arms and legs. And then he noticed the peace of her sleep. The unconscious safety from the real world that had closed in and confused her and he felt the same thing. The closing in. The confusion. He admired her now slack expression and with her change he saw her differently than he had seen her at any moment since she had appeared from the dark. She had become more human and he envied her sleep and he tried to imagine the bliss of her bewilderment. He reached down and picked away a leaf that was stuck in her hair and then he plucked a twig poking from her housecoat.

The ringing stopped.

What did you know, he wanted to ask her. What called you into the night? What guided you through the dark? Is there something that gives you the answers the rest of us cannot know?

Burdean called him again. Keal looked out of the window. Ed was crawling out of the truck bed and returning behind the wheel. Burdean stood in front of the truck and stared at the little girl through the windshield. Keal brushed a curl of hair back from the old woman's forehead. He then reached into his coat pocket and took out the two rolls of cash he had taken from her in the passage of the night and he lifted her hand that lay on her chest and tucked them underneath. He walked out of the house as the telephone began to ring again.

10

The four silent souls came upon the abandoned big car after only minutes back on the road. Ed let them out and the passenger door was still closing when he hit the gas and sped away. Keal and Burdean and the little girl stood there and watched the truck disappear and then the sound of the engine faded and the morning birds sang to them in earnest.

The men turned and looked at her at the same time. The little girl was darkhaired and darkeyed and there was a birthmark over her right temple that had the resemblance of a butterfly from one angle and the glare of a bird of prey from another. She wore a denim jacket that seemed to cover several layers of shirts. Her hair fell parted down the middle and was cut lopsided just above her shoulders. She held her hands in the pockets of her jacket and she stared back at the men with rigidity. As if she had gathered as much stubbornness as she could gather in her young life and there was nowhere else to carry it but in the bend of her brow.

"How old are you?" Keal said.

"Fuck that," Burdean said. "What were you doing out there in that old church?"

"Slow down, Burdean."

"You slow down."

Burdean pulled a pack of cigarettes from his pocket and tapped one out and lit it. He began to walk a circle in the road, mumbling to himself.

Keal leaned down to meet the girl's eyes.

"Are you all right? Are you hurt?"

She didn't budge.

"What's your name?"

He may as well have been talking to a tree. Keal raised up and walked away from her and he held out his hand and Burdean gave him a cigarette.

"She looks about eight or nine don't you think?" Keal said.

"Yep."

"She look hurt to you?"

"Of course she looks hurt. Goddamn kid hid away in the black of a cellar with a bunch of dead men laying around."

"You didn't have no idea?"

Burdean took a long drag and looked over at the child. She was tracing her finger around the outline of her birthmark, moving it perfectly as if she was looking at it in a reflection. Then he looked back to Keal and said I didn't have no idea and I mean it. I've done a lot of shit that ain't upstanding but transporting children ain't one of them.

She coughed. Wiped her nose on the sleeve of her jacket.

"She looks scared," Keal said.

"She looks mad."

"She's probably a lot of things. What you think?"

Burdean smoked. Spit and wiped at his whiskers. The lines around his eyes bent in thought.

"I think she must be important."

"What does that mean?"

"You saw what I saw," Burdean said. "It's clearly more than one of us trying to get ahold of her."

"Important how?"

"I don't know, Keal. You're seeing what I'm seeing and it's impressed upon me."

Keal put the cigarette in the corner of his mouth but did not light it.

"Let's try talking to her again," Burdean said.

"Fine. But don't start cussing."

The men crossed the road back to her. She was standing in the same spot. Staring in the same direction, toward the brim of the rising sun that was dusting the east in pink. This time Keal knelt on one knee in front of her. He tried to remember the way his mother used to talk to him when he was a boy but before he could speak she reached and took the unlit cigarette from his mouth as if that would help him. Her eyes held on him with such conviction that he became unsettled. As if she should be asking the questions and he should be giving the answers. But he started anyway.

What is your name? Do you know where you are? Are you hurt or injured? Where is your family? Do you have a family? Do you know who brought you to the cellar? Is there somewhere you want us to take you? Someone you want us to call? The questions were short and basic, with pauses in between to allow for her to respond and all of them went unanswered. Keal raised from his knee. Burdean only smoked and mumbled to himself. Then Keal knelt again and asked her if she spoke English. Then he pointed at his ears and at her ears and asked if she could hear.

Without a word or change in expression she handed the cigarette back to Keal.

"This keeps getting better," Burdean said.

Keal lit the cigarette and stood with Burdean. Inhales and exhales and indecision. The girl folded her arms.

"Did you see that shit painted on the walls of that room under there?" Keal said.

Burdean nodded. He pulled a phone from his coat pocket and looked at it. Missed call after missed call after missed call.

"Maybe I should just bite the bullet and call back and see what we were supposed to do with her."

"Maybe not."

"Maybe," Burdean said.

"Maybe you could call and say there wasn't nothing there."

"Yeah. And then what?"

Neither of them had an answer.

"Besides," Burdean said. "I'm guessing it's way too late for that lie."

"How you think that old woman found her?" Keal said.

Burdean flicked his cigarette into the road and he laughed and then huffed and said if you're waiting on me to figure out anything that's happened since I picked you up yesterday then you might as well get comfortable somewhere because there are no such explanations forthcoming. He then put the phone away.

The girl moved. She opened the car door and sat down on the benchseat and she picked up the crayon drawing of the angel and sat looking at it.

"I do however figure this."

"What?" Keal said.

"I never once in my whole life believed there was weird shit in the dark and I sure as hell thought I was too old to believe in such. But there is something in these woods. Something I don't really feel like finding out more about. And the longer we sit right here in this spot the better the odds that somebody is gonna come down this road that we don't want to meet."

11

The old woman's phone kept ringing as the sun peeked over the edge of the horizon and it rang as the sun rose higher and burned away the morning mist that dampened the countryside. It rang as the birds began to sing and as the deer crossed the yard and it rang as the morning breeze pushed a wind chime and it rang as the mail truck puttered along the road and stopped and the postman shoved more into the stuffed mailbox and it kept ringing until the sun was high and yellow and sitting atop the sky and then it stopped. A family of raccoons sat on their haunches and stared at the phone on the wall and listened to it ring before turning their attention back to the paradise of the littered kitchen.

The old woman slept like the dead in the recliner.

A skinny brown dog came trotting along the road and loped into the yard. It sniffed around and then it climbed the front steps. Poked its head into the open doorway. Its eyes watery and nose in quick little jolts of discovery. It was careful as it stepped inside. Waiting to be harangued by a hard voice or swatted with a hard hand. But there was only the snoring from the old woman. And the smells of decay that no dog could resist.

It navigated the heaps. Raising its leg to piss on the base of a floor lamp. Sticking its nose into an empty shoebox. It sniffed on through the house until it arrived at the kitchen and the floor was covered in trash and food scraps and when the dog stepped into the kitchen the blackeyed creatures dropped what they were doing and they bared their teeth and hissed in a rabid chorus and the dog was familiar with what it was like to fight a raccoon much less a pack of raccoons and it slunk back out of the kitchen and out of the house carrying its hunger.

The dog lay down in the yard. Stretched its gangly limbs and then settled into a sundrenched slumber and it was still in the same position underneath a clear and cool sky when the Volkswagen pulled into the driveway.

12

She wore Jesus around her neck in the form of a six-inch crucifix that could be and had been used as a weapon. The wooden crucifix had been a garage sale pickup and it hung from a crimson ribbon that matched the thornpunctured forehead of Christ and the bottom of the cross had been cracked in a roadhouse ruckus that left the groping man on his knees and bent over with his head on the floor as if he were pausing to pray instead of ending up on the backside of touching the wrong woman in the wrong place at the wrong time.

Cara got out of the Volkswagen and looked at the dog. It raised its head from the ground and regarded her a lazy moment before returning to its grassy cushion. She then noticed the front door open. She crossed the yard and stood in the threshold and called out.

"Miss Wanetah?"

She leaned in and saw the old woman sleeping in the recliner.

She then noticed the scratches on her face and feet and scraps of the woods stuck in her hair and on her housecoat. She stood over her and she was so still that Cara thought she might be dead but then she snorted and turned on her side and remained hard asleep. When she turned the two rolls of cash slipped from beneath her hand and rolled off the pile and dropped onto the floor.

Cara watched them tumble. Then she looked around the room as if someone may be watching to take notice of how she would react. She picked them up and held a roll in each hand as if to measure their weight against one another. Wondering where they came from. Wondering if there was more. And then she began to imagine the old woman cat burgling the countryside, wearing her dementia as a disguise while she sensibly robbed the country folk. Climbing in and out of windows. Picking the locks of gun safes. Lifting cash from wallets and purses while dinner was being had in the other room. One roll had a wipe of blood on the outer bill. The other looked as if it had been kicked around in the dirt.

She heard the rustling from the kitchen and she set the rolls on the recliner next to Wanetah. When she stepped into the kitchen she saw the raccoons and called them all sons of bitches and she scooped up a chair and fought back their hissing and gnashing as if she was standing center ring under the big top and taming the lions. She drove the raccoons into the corner and she opened the kitchen door and they did not go easy but they finally fled the animated woman wielding the chair and cussing with conviction.

Cara shut the door. She set the chair down and sat in it. She surveyed the mess of the kitchen and then she dropped her head in sympathy. The crucifix swayed as she leaned forward. The color of her hair varied with the seasons and it was somewhere between blond and brown with streaks of burgundy, streaks she had colored out of boredom and the burgundy fell in waves around her eyes and along the curve of her neck and she rubbed her hands together as if they needed to be warmed.

She lived a mile away. No other houses between them. She and the old woman separated by two bends in the road and a hundred patched potholes and barbed wire and wildflowers. She had not known the woman until the last year, noticing Wanetah sitting in a lawn chair in the yard. Doing nothing but just sitting there. Cara had begun by waving to her and then she started to stop when she saw her and sometimes Wanetah remembered her name and sometimes she didn't. There were days when the two women sat together and spoke of the world with rich clarity and there were other days when it seemed as if they were discussing a riddle that could not be solved.

Some days it felt like the same thing.

Cara knew the old woman was deteriorating in mind and body but even on the days of lucidity Cara could not find the detail she needed. The name of a sister or child or nurse or friend or anyone who seemed to be helping or who seemed to be part of her life in even the smallest of ways. So she had made Wanetah part of her routine in recent months. Bringing her groceries and calling to check on her and stopping by to see her when she was both going and coming. The old woman had been in the long clutch of dementia since before they had met but the deterioration of recent weeks had come on with the thrust of finality and the increase of hoarding and the mess of the house ran parallel with her decline.

Cara sat up straight in the chair. Realizing it was time to do something. She pushed the sleeves of her sweatshirt to her elbows. She crossed her legs, her knee poking through the rip in her jeans.

She didn't know why but she had awakened in the middle of the night with Wanetah stuck in her mind. A thought so forceful it was as if the old woman may have been standing at the foot of her bed and she sat up halfexpecting to see her there. Overcome with the impulse that the old woman was somewhere she shouldn't have been. Cara had risen from the bed and paced around in the dark in her t-shirt and bare feet, trying to rid herself of the falling feeling that comes with the suspicion of bad news. She had paced and turned the television on and off and washed the dishes in the sink and written a letter to a man she had loved briefly and watched the clock turn two and then three and then four before she finally lay back down and settled herself in the belief that she was only stuck in the middle of a bad dream and not awake with intuition. Then she fell asleep in the final hour before dawn, missing the gunshots that echoed across the hill country.

She had called Wanetah the instant she woke up. She made coffee and called again and then she went to work at the gas station and rang up sausage biscuits and tater logs and cups of coffee for working men who piled into working trucks and she called several times from behind the counter and then she finally left and drove back out to check on her. And she had been right. The old woman had been somewhere she wasn't supposed to be. She didn't know how far she had wandered off into the woods but she had wandered off into the woods and it seemed nothing less than a miracle that the old woman was now asleep in the house. She believed Wanetah would die in some awful way if left alone. Fallen and hurt and scared either inside the house or in a gulley in the woods or hit by a car in the depths of night that would never see her in time to stop as she walked in the middle of the road searching for something that was years or decades in the past.

Or maybe the old woman would only lie down in the same spot she was in right now, on a pile of her own clothes in her own recliner in her own house and die right where she was supposed to die while she slept and traveled through a pleasant dream of youth on her way to the other side.

How do you know?

Cara stood from the chair and walked back outside. The raccoons were gone. So was the dog. She trailed her fingers along the ribbon of the crucifix. How do you know about your own life, she thought. Much less the life of someone else.

She then reached into her pocket and she pulled out a lock of hair, tied at each end with pieces of string. She set the lock in the palm of her hand and it lay in a curl and she stroked the tip of her finger along its softness. She then closed her hand and the lock was both weightless and heavy and her eyes trailed across the countryside and she watched the leaves fall from the trees in the morning wind. She tucked the lock back into her pocket and then tried to gauge which movement she would regret the least. Making a phone call that would have people arrive and take Wanetah away for her own safety to live in some other place with others like her where the walls were painted in white or green and the doors were locked and the meals were delivered at regular hours and the strangeness of her life would shrink into a small room with hopefully a window. Or she could let her be. And when the day came that the old woman disappeared and became a ghost of the land then she could do what she had done in the previous moments of her life when the brutality of the world had delivered her into the shadows. Drink a bottle of wine and maybe another bottle of wine and pretend she didn't see it coming.

13

They decided to take the girl to a place that Burdean knew of. A place where he had hidden himself away when previous jobs had called for disappearing for a day or two or three. A place where they could sit and rest and hope that some combination of time and fate could deliver the answer they needed.

The ninety-year-old hotel faced the railroad tracks and once upon a time men and women had sat on the balcony that was an extension of the second floor restaurant and sipped gin and dined on shrimp and redfish. When the train made its stop, passengers stepped off for a smalltown pause in the back and forth between Chicago and New Orleans, unable to resist the seductive hotel they had seen from the train car window. The chandelier glistened in the foyer and ferns grew grand and green in enormous terra-cotta pots outside the handcarved doors. The hotel seemed like a postcard. An elegant structure where both memories and secrets had been made in the transformative hours between cocktails and sleep.

It was not like that anymore.

The bottom floor was part pool hall, mostly pawn shop. The remnants of sophistication long since painted over or torn out or laid over with linoleum. Wood paneling and a door had hidden away the mahogany staircase and a dustcovered globe of buttery light hung from the ceiling where the chandelier once gave a starlight twinkle. The upstairs could only be reached by climbing a set of metal grate stairs attached to the outside of the building and the weary groan of each step served as an illtoned warning for the redeyed patrons of the hotel rooms that were now one-room flops that could be paid for in cash or flesh or some other agreed upon trade.

Burdean had made a deal with the pawn shop owner and bought a key to the room at the end of the hall. And then he had bought a padlock. And each time he had needed the room he expected the door frame to be busted and he expected to find a strange smell or a strange body sprawled across the bed but each time he found the room like he had left it. Unoccupied and littered with his own mess and slightly better smelling than the passage of the hallway.

The room was sparse with only a bed and three folding chairs. Ageless wallpaper clung to the walls decorated with the faint pattern of the fleur-de-lis. A wad of pillows and blankets covered the bed and a checkerboard was open on a milk crate between two of the folding chairs, Burdean in competition with himself to pass the hiding hours of the random visits. The closet door was open and a bottle of Old Forester and a carton of cigarettes sat on the top shelf and a garbage can overflowing with empty beer cans sat beneath the large window that looked into the alleyway. When they came into the room hours before, Burdean told Keal I know you don't sleep and don't like to sleep but I got to sleep. You sit here and listen and watch and then we'll trade. Burdean took a blanket and pillow from the bed and he laid it out on the scarred wooden floor and he pointed to the bed and told the girl she could have it if she wanted it.

She had sat down on the edge of the bed and watched Burdean settle down on his pallet and within minutes he had fallen into a deep sleep. Keal sat in a folding chair by the window. He asked her if she was hungry and she ran her eyes across the foodless room as if to say what exactly would I eat if I was. The girl eventually eased herself up onto the bed. She unbuttoned her denim coat and when she did she slipped out the framed crayon angel. She held it with both hands and studied it and then she traced the roughly drawn wings. Then she raised her finger and made the same tracing motion with her index finger. Keal asked her if she liked the drawing but she did not answer. She set the frame aside and she scooted back on the bed and laid her head on a pillow and stretched out on top of the remaining blanket. She lay with her arms folded and her eyes on the ceiling and Keal gave up trying to talk to her.

An air of exhaustion filled the room. Voices and knocks came from somewhere down the hallway in a morning ruckus. Voices that grew louder and louder until there was a crash. Keal thought he heard someone crying but the sobbing faded away before he could decide if it was real and the upstairs returned to silence. A train whistle sounded from way down the tracks.

When he looked again at the girl her eyes were closed and her folded arms had relented and fallen to her sides. Her stoic expression had faded and he thought for the first time that she looked like a child was supposed to look.

Sit here and listen and watch.

He moved the chair across the room, away from the window and against the wall. He leaned back and stretched out his legs. He picked up a checker from the checkerboard and passed it back and forth in his hands and then he laid his head back on the wall. The fatigue came over him in a single breath. His mind and his body relenting. There was nothing to watch for out of the window except for the gathering of blackbirds on the rooftop of the building across the alley so he rested his eyes and though there was a whirlwind of thought tearing through his mind and though he was not expecting it or wanting to he somehow fell asleep. The checker fell from his slack hand and ticked on the floor.

He dreamed straightaway.

He walked along the trodden path of a countryside where big clouds moved like glaciers and a raven circled above and there was only the sound of the wind pushing through the trees in the tranquil sway of a peaceful day. The path led into a clearing and the land began to slope and the clouds gathered and turned from white to gray as the ground beneath his feet became soggy and sucked at his feet as he continued on toward a gathering of trees that were losing their color and then their leaves in a timewarp change of the seasons. A gentle and sound-less rain began to fall and he stood bewildered by the hush of it all and he held out his hands and turned his face to the sky and he savored the rain in the strange sensation of baptism and just as he felt as if the heavens were holding him in some special way, a thunderclap busted the silence and the wind began to whip around him and the rain stopped and left him with the feeling of abandonment in the everdarkening world. The clouds grew black and were pushed across the leaden sky by heavy winds and the thunder rolled in overlapping clamor and then just as quickly as the storm had gathered and risen, the wind stopped and the thunder stopped.

The dream grew as still as a photograph. A black and white image of a time and place asking to be remembered. Keal stood inside the dream as if waiting on a message to be delivered.

A single strike of lightning fractured the sky. And then there came another and another as the lightning flashed against the dark in a chaotic mess as if in celebration of its own power. Keal watched, mesmerized by the destructive beauty. A performance of the gods. He was drawn and he walked with admiration in the direction of the lightning storm when a great flash revealed the silhouette of a building. Big and rectangular and as black as the sky. Then the lightning began to strike against the earth, sending treetops into a fiery blaze and blowing craters into the countryside and Keal began to run toward the building in hopes of shelter, panicked and ducking and dodging and he was almost there when the whitehot bolt struck the roof and the building erupted into flames.

He woke with a jolt. Nearly falling out of the folding chair. He caught himself and he wiped at his face and rubbed at his eyes and when he fully regained reality, he looked across the room and the little girl was standing in front of the window. The sunlight that warmed the room had disappeared and the sky had grown overcast. She stood in the ashen light and stared at the clouds with hardshell conviction, the trail of a purple vein ran crooked down her forehead and pulsed right through her birthmark. And her hands were raised to her chest and clenched in whiteknuckled fists as if she may be conjuring the power of God.

14

Keal waited and watched the girl as she stood with her eyes locked on the sky and her small body held taut until she finally relented. The vein disappeared and she lowered her eyes and her cheeks rose in a long exhale. Then she unclenched her fists. She looked at her hands and flexed her fingers. Her shoulders had been held back as if in military attention and they lost their intensity and slumped forward. A roll of thunder crossed the sky. She turned and looked at Keal with an air of deflation. A strand of hair slipped right between her eyes and fell over her nose and mouth. She raised her hand methodically and her flateyed expression never changed as she took the strand and moved it behind her ear.

Burdean hadn't budged. Asleep on his back with his arm tucked behind his head.

Keal stood from the chair and he put on his coat. Burdean had set the car keys on the closet shelf next to the carton of cigarettes and Keal took them and was turning for the door when she crossed the room and met him there.

"You stay here," he told her.

She shook her head.

"I won't be gone long. Just wait."

Her dark eyes held him and there was no use in arguing. He nodded to her and opened the door. She grabbed the framed angel from the bed and they walked out into the hallway together.

Keal believed Burdean. There was something in those woods. There was something at that church. And there was hellfire sure something about this girl and he was going back to see what it was all about without Burdean there to temper his imagination. He had wanted to do it alone but now the girl was with him and her presence gave him a strange calm he did not expect. As they walked along the sidewalk and then climbed into the car the clouds separated again and revealed pockets of blue sky and as the reborn sun spilled into the day, he was overcome with the sensation that this little girl had somehow seen or been responsible for the lightning of his dreams.

15

Cara woke the old woman. The old woman sat up in the recliner and did not know who she was or where they were and Cara was both dismayed by the depths of Wanetah's confusion and relieved that the decision of what to do seemed to have been made for her.

She called the gas station and told them she wouldn't be coming back. And then she dialed 911 because she didn't know what other number you call to ask for help for an old woman lost in the recesses of her own mind. What came next was her astonishment at the brevity with which it all happened. As if there was a team whose sole responsibility was to rescue the aged from solitude and confusion and they sat around a table staring at a red lamp like firefighters waiting on a fire. Within an hour Wanetah's house was filled with a woman from social services and two more women from a hospice facility and an emergency medic who pulled up in an ambulance with the siren screaming for reasons Cara did not understand. Cara answered whatever questions she could answer and then she watched them try to talk to Wanetah. The old woman couldn't remember her own name and Cara imagined Wanetah's last bits of reality drifting somewhere in the wind. Lost in the wandering night. A final plummet into complete darkness.

Cara watched them take her blood pressure and try to identify the random bottles of pills scattered from the kitchen to the bathroom and Cara helped them dig through a drawer full of documents in her bedroom in an effort to figure out her full name and her social security number and if she had bank accounts and if she had any insurance that mattered. Cara helped the hospice workers find clean clothes and shoes and a suitcase to pack it all in and while this was going on around her Wanetah sat on a stack of outdated phone books in the corner of the living room with one knobby knee crossed over the other as if in perfect understanding and acceptance of what was going on around her. The social worker finally knelt in front of the old woman and the team stood behind her as the social worker explained to Wanetah that it was time to leave. That she was going to have a new place to live and she would be taken care of and she would be safe and Wanetah sat speechless through the explanation until the woman finally asked her if she had any questions of her own.

"Yes," the old woman said.

"What is it?"

Wanetah put her hand to her mouth. Ran her fingertips across her chapped lips and she sank into some deeper thought before she leaned forward and her eyes widened as if she had been suddenly disturbed.

"Can you keep her from the edge of the world?"

They all looked at one another. And then they looked at Cara who only shook her head in sadness and then watched with the others as Wanetah rose from the stack of phone books. She held out her wrinkled hand to be led away by strangers.

16

Cara had spent a decade and a half searching for her own haven. She had come from a big family. Five brothers and sisters and grandparents and eight aunts and uncles and more cousins than names she could remember and she never connected with or much liked any of them. They had all lived in mobile homes within ten acres of one another, separated only by the pine trees of southeast Mississippi and the beaten paths made by four-wheelers and it had always felt more like a manufactured compound of bloodlines and closeknit personalities than a collection of individuals capable of finding their own way. Even as a child she came to anticipate what someone was going to say before they said it. And the tone of voice they would say it with. And who or what they would say it about. There were always too many people coming and going. Always cousins right up under her when she wanted to be left alone. Always a cluster of them gathered at the bus stop that the other kids laughed at.

The only soulful connection she believed existed was a grandmother who decided she couldn't take the mob of family anymore and she had moved away when Cara was a teenager. She had left the pines and driven four hours away into the north Mississippi hill country and paid cash for a meager four-room house in the woods. She had returned only once, coerced into returning into the pines for a Fourth of July family cookout and the last thing Cara remembered her grandmother saying before she got in her Buick to leave the morning after was if you got any sense and I know you do, you'll get away from all this nonsense. There is a vacuum out here that will suck you down into the pit of the earth. There is something different about you, Cara. Something special. Her grandmother then handed her a plastic bag filled with notepads and pens and a box of envelopes and stamps and they spent Cara's teenage years writing back and forth to one another. The days Cara spent writing to her grandmother and going to the mailbox in anticipation of her grandmother's reply helped the time go by. And through the relationship of words, her grandmother helped to forge a strength in Cara.

When she turned eighteen, she found herself brave enough to leave. Her dad gave her his fourteen-year-old pickup as her high school graduation present and she promptly loaded it up and headed for the coast. She spent a few years waiting tables at the casinos or at crabshacks and then she grew bored with the sand and she left for Jackson and spent a couple more years pouring beer and whiskey at a pub. She moved in and out of similar apartments in similar parts of town and wherever she lived sirens filled the nights and she could not walk alone but none of it bothered or mattered to her. Each apartment was her own place paid for with her own money and her own silence to return to at the end of a shift. She had her own phone with her own number. She could wear her hair any color she liked. She had her own decisions to make and her own people to let into her life and the pines grew as distant as the discolored twinkle of another planet. She felt free and she was filled with the idea that something special was coming her way. Just like her grandmother had always told her. And then she met Madrid and Lola.

She had left the pub and started working in a coffeehouse and on a rainy morning, a young woman about her age and her two-year-old daughter came in and sat down. In the middle of the coffeehouse was a table with crayons and coloring sheets and the woman got the toddler situated and entertained enough for her to come to the counter and ask for an application. Her name was Madrid and she was tall and her black hair hung in thick curls across her shoulders and down her back and the toddler had the same shiny black curls that fell down the sides of her face. Cara had given Madrid an application and introduced her to the manager and a week later Madrid started working there.

Madrid had left her east Texas home for reasons worse than Cara had for fleeing the pines. On the days they worked together they would walk down the street after their shift to a hole of a pizza shop where they would eat slices and tell each other about their lives. Madrid downplayed the poverty she had run away from but when she talked about the steps in the journey between home and here there was no mistaking the toll. Her brown eyes turned to the wall or down to the floor and she rubbed at a scar on the back of her hand. Each time that the story would make its way to the arrival of Lola, Cara watched her sink deeper into her realizations about the world she and the child navigated. There was hunger on its edge. And there was nothing worse than hunger, Madrid had said more than once. In the voice of someone who knew. The two women recognized one another as wanderers and when Cara asked Madrid to move in with her where they could share the bills and share the care of Lola, Madrid brushed the thick curls back from her face and nodded and smiled and reached for Cara's hand.

It had worked for almost a year. Friendship and a notion of family. And then Madrid began to ask Cara to stay with Lola so she could go out by herself at night. And then she found excuses to not go into work at the coffeehouse. She would only tell Cara she was going out with friends but she never introduced the friends to Cara and never brought them around the apartment but Cara minded less than she expected because she had fallen in love with Madrid's daughter. In the mother's absence, Cara and Lola watched cartoons in the evening and sometimes went out for ice cream and on her days off she took Lola to the library and they would check out a stack of books and Cara read to her and Lola sat mesmerized at the stories and the illustrations and Cara sang songs to her at bedtime to help her fall asleep when her mother wasn't there. And then sometimes Madrid would go out and not come back to the apartment until the next morning. And then her disappearances increased and she would be gone for two or three days at a time. Her thin frame had grown thinner and her brown eyes had lost their luster and when Cara finally challenged her about where she had been and what she had been doing and who she had been doing it with she only walked wordlessly into her bedroom and closed and locked the door. On the day that Cara returned to the apartment after work and the babysitter handed her a note that Madrid had instructed her to give to Cara, she was not surprised when it read PLEASE TAKE CARE OF LOLA.

She had sat down the next morning and written a long letter to her grandmother explaining the predicament she was in. But by the end of the letter she had come around to the notion that it was not a dilemma but instead what she had been meant for. You always said I was special, she wrote. Now I can be special for someone else even though I know how hard this is going to be.

But she didn't know.

There was nothing she could do when half a year later Madrid returned. Cleareyed. Weight on her bones. A set of car keys dangling from her hand as she told Cara she had made her mistakes and now she was back and she was taking Lola with her. Thank you for what you did. Lola sat next to Cara on the couch as Madrid paced back and forth and acted as if she was in some kind of hurry and when Cara tried to argue she grew obstinate that you are not her mother and I am and she is going with me and that's it. Madrid had then knelt in front of Lola and gave her excuses in one breath and assurance in the next and then she had hurriedly thrown some of Lola's clothes and a few toys into a bag and she slung the bag over her shoulder and she picked up the little girl who was calling for Cara and Madrid jerked away from Cara's grip on her arm and then they were down the apartment stairs and into a car where a man sat behind the wheel and they were gone. And so was everything. All the trips to the playground and the park and all the lazy evenings with coloring books and macaroni and cheese and all the moments of learning the names of colors and shapes and the recognition of letters and using new words and all the moments when the little girl would start talking and she wouldn't stop in the joy and exploration of her own interpretations and imaginings of her little life and all the quiet moments when Cara had told her that she was loved.

Can you keep her from the edge of the world?

She did not know who Wanetah was talking about but it made no difference. She understood.

17

The church looked different in the daylight. Even with the carnage. With the chirps and calls of the surrounding woods and with the squirrels darting across the sagging roof and with the sunshine reflecting on the dingy stainedglass the old church carried the illusion that it may still be capable of resurrecting. Keal and the girl sat in the car and looked out at the four dead men who had been propped up and sat next to one another on the front steps in their bloodsoaked shirts and appeared to be in the comradery of a midday nap instead of growing cold and stiff. The van and the truck remained in the same spots with the same doors open. The cellar remained open and the scene had given Keal all he needed to be convinced to put the big car in reverse and leave though he wouldn't.

The girl got out of the car. Keal called to her but she kept going and then he climbed out, the pistol in his coat pocket. She walked over to the four men and stood in front of them. Tilted her head in a study of their morbid expressions.

"Do you know them?" Keal said. "Quienes son?"

She took a step closer. Keal looked around, wondering if whoever had moved the men was still there. Wondering if someone or something may rise out of the cellar. The girl stepped closer to the lineup and she reached down and lifted the wrist of the man on the end and she slipped a braided cloth bracelet from his wrist. Then she put it on her own wrist and turned to Keal and pointed at herself.

"It's yours. I get it. That should solve everything."

She walked away from Keal and the dead men and returned to the car.

Keal reached into his pocket and gripped the pistol. He then explored the inside of the van and the inside of the truck. He searched under seats and inside gloveboxes and flipped down visors and there was nothing that helped. The girl sat on the hood of the car with her eyes on the dead as if they may rise again. He looked back at her in indecision before walking over to the open doors of the cellar. The sunlight spilled down into the opening and seeped into the dark. Keal moved down the stairs. Two steps and stop and listen. Two more steps and stop and listen. This way until the bottom.

The cellar turned gray with the reach of daylight and Keal saw the same things he had seen with Burdean's flashlight. Three decaying bodies on the floor. The bones of small animals. A snakeskin. The door at the other end. He wanted to go into the room with the markings on the wall where they had found the girl but the kerosene lamp had long since burned out and the deeper into the cellar the greater the dark. He remembered the cigarette lighter in his pocket and he pulled it out and flicked it. He crept along with the paltry flame and was a step away from the door when he heard the thud of a car door closing.

He looked back over his shoulder toward the stairs. Thinking. It is the girl getting in the car. It is the girl getting in the car.

Another thud. Then the blare of a car horn.

He dropped the lighter and ran for the stairs, up and out and back into the light and as he ran around the side of the church he saw a sedan parked behind the big car and two men pulled on locked door handles as the girl sat in the middle of the benchseat with her hands pressed against her temples. Keal fired a shot into the air and the men ducked. Didn't run but raised back up with their own pistols and fired on him. Keal jumped in the side door of the van and the back window exploded. He lifted his head enough to see them coming toward the van and he fired through the open window and one of the men went down and the other darted off to the right and out of his sight and he was shifting to the front seat when he saw the little girl climb out of the car and take off running down the road. Bullets pocked the van and he dropped to the ribbed floor and cussed and crawled between the driver and passenger seats. Then the shots stopped.

He expected to lift his eyes and see the man staring at him through the windshield but when he looked up he was not there. Keal raised and searched and didn't see him anywhere and then he hustled to the back window and looked toward the road and he saw the man running in the direction of the girl. He leapt out of the side door and ran for the big car. Cranking it and spinning in the churchyard and then spinning in the gravel and his wheels caught the road with a shriek.

18

Cara helped load Wanetah into the car and then she watched them drive away from the old woman's house with the ambulance following. She touched the bulge of the two rolls of cash in the pocket of her jeans. Trying not to question anything that had been done. She had been in this space before, when in an instant a place can be changed forever. The sound and the feel and the personality of years or even decades gone with one mighty and fatal blow. When the countryside was quiet again she did what she always did in the daylight hours when she was alone and without answers. She got in the Volkswagen and lit a cigarette and went lowriding through the backroads.

The Volkswagen was yellow with rust around the edges of the windshield and a convertible top that was worn ragged with age and miles and it flapped in a clumsy rhythm she no longer noticed. She turned off the radio. Never wanting anything but the bumps and sways and sights in her backroad therapy. She drove in a lull. Easy up and over the hills and around the curves, a hawk sitting on a fencepost and a doe grazing and the burnt colors of autumn and the leaves on the road rising behind her in little whirlwinds and then falling again. She made turns at crossroads without thought or reason to direction. Her mind drifting. Sometimes wondering if the things that had happened to her had really happened to her. Sometimes envious of Wanctah's unknowing. The old woman will be fine, she thought. She doesn't have much distance to go. What about those of us who do?

Or think we do.

She tossed her cigarette butt out of the window and then held her left hand raised before her. Looked at the pinky and ring fingers that had been bent and broken and now stood crooked as if in defiance of the others. They did not wiggle like the others. Did not move or grip like the others. They ached when the weather was right.

She came around the treelined bend and slammed on the brakes and jerked the wheel as she damn near hit the child who was running down the middle of the road. The Volkswagen skidded off the asphalt and slid in the rocks and dirt but kept out of the ditch as Cara yanked it back onto the road and came to a hard stop. She was sitting there catching her breath and yelling what the shit when a man with a pistol came running past and she put the simple puzzle together and she shifted into reverse trying to get turned around and she threw it into first gear just as the big car swung around the bend and caught the rear end, spinning her around and ripping off the bumper and the big car swerved and squealed and there was the clamor of damn near vehicular death but the big car kept going. The Volkswagen was still running and she gathered herself in an instant and could only see that child running from whatever the hell this all was and she shifted into gear and chased after.

She saw them ahead along a quartermile of straightaway. The big car zoomed past the running man who fired on the car, a succession of pop pop pops. But the big car kept on and caught up to the girl, who had left the road and was ducking between the wooden rails of a fence and the child kept running across a pasture as the driver jumped out of the big car and raced after her. Cara shifted gears and gained speed and the running man in the road turned and raised his pistol on her and she never slowed down, the windshield splitting with the bullet and the man knew he was in for it and he jumped just as the Volkswagen met him with a great whack, flipping him into the air and Cara swerving but holding on and she saw him bounce and break in the rearview mirror.

She slammed to a stop next to the big car, tiresmoke wafting past her as she got out and followed them across the fence and into the pasture. Forty yards behind. She could hear the man calling out for the child to stop and he waved his arms though she was not looking back and he was gaining on her and Cara did not know what she would do when she got to them but she was about to find out as the man ran the girl down and caught her with both of his arms and lifted her off the ground in a big squeeze and the child kicked and flailed but he held her tight. By the time Cara caught up the child had quit kicking and the man carried her back in the direction of the road, talking to her and telling her to hold still. It's all right. Hold still and don't take off running just be still. We have to get out of here.

Cara met them with both her good hand and her bad hand ready to fight but before she could say or do anything Keal asked her where he was.

"Who?"

"The other guy."

"I hit him."

"Hit him with what?"

"My car."

Keal hustled on. Breathing hard and losing his grip on the girl and stopping and hoisting her into a better hold and then moving on and Cara hustled right beside them and then she grabbed his arm and pulled him to a stop.

"What the hell are you doing?" she said.

"Let go."

She tried to wrench his arms from the child.

"I'm the good guy," he yelled and they stood there wrestling and grunting as she tried to pry the girl free and she asked the girl if she was hurt and if she knew this man or if she had ever seen him before and Keal couldn't hold the girl any longer with Cara pulling at his arms and he set the girl down but clamped his hand on the back of her jacket.

"This ain't what you think," he said.

"Tell me," she said to the girl.

"She won't answer."

"Like hell."

"I'm telling you this ain't what you think."

"Then what is it."

Keal then held up his hand. Asking for a pause. His ear turned to the road.

"Listen," he said.

The hum of a vehicle. They all looked toward the road and the sedan was making its way toward them. Keal grabbed the girl by the arm and ran, the girl dragging some and running some and Cara fell in behind them and had no more questions but only followed them back to the fence and through the fence and the sedan had stopped at the man lying still in the road. Keal opened the door and shoved the child into the car and he turned to Cara and said if I was you I'd get your ass in here. The sedan started again and sped toward them and Cara ran around and got in the passenger side and the door was still open when Keal stomped the gas and the big car lurched and the door slammed shut with the momentum.

Keal drove fast and sloppy, on and off the road and sliding around the country curves and the girl knocking back and forth between Cara and Keal as the sedan gained on them and then just as quickly as it gained the sedan began to lag behind. And drift. And Keal knew it had to be the man he shot and he had to be bleeding out and he looked over his shoulder as the sedan slowed and veered off the road and settled harmlessly into the thick brush at the edge of the woods.

19

Burdean marched up and down the sidewalk in front of the flophouse, chainsmoking and swearing that if he ever laid eyes on Keal again he would beat him into a puddle. Not shoot him or kill him but beat the everlivingdogshit out of him and leave him laid out in the middle of nowhere for the vultures to peck on because he was certain that Keal was thinking the same thing Burdean was thinking. That girl is important and important things are worth something and with each cigarette Burdean became more convinced that Keal had suckered him and had carried her off in search of a payday. With who he didn't know and if Keal had such a connection he was sure as hell more savvy than he'd given him credit for being. He had been hustled and in his outlaw mind that was the worst thing you could be. It was the only way he knew how to think. That little shit.

Burdean started walking. The railroad tracks divided the

small town that was made up of bricked streets and weathered facades and old buildings that clung to their charm against age and apathy. The sidewalks were empty and only the random car was parked along the street. He came to a bank that was boarded up, all but the teller window and a spraypainted arrow along the side of the building directed customers to it. A one-show cinema announced DBL FEATR ATURDAY on the marquee. Crepe myrtles grew from whiskey barrels on the corner of each block. He walked and nodded when the random townfolk passed by.

He went inside a smoke store and bought a pack of cigarettes and spent a minute trying to process all the new and different things to smoke and all the new and different devices to smoke them with and he wondered what was wrong with the simplicity of a lighter and a cigarette. He headed back toward the flophouse but paused at his favorite building. An old gin distillery with a collapsed roof. The equipment had rusted and fallen through the rotted floor and vines had climbed into the building from some-where and twisted through the wreckage as if trying to wrap it up and keep it from descending further into ruin. Burdean thought it looked something like a shipwreck illustration from a book he had read as a boy. He smoked and watched a swarm of gnats appear from a hole beneath the broken floorplanks and then he heard the big car coming and he walked back along the street and stood in front of the pawn shop door with his arms crossed in aggravation.

When the big car turned the corner a block away, Burdean saw the bullet holes in the windshield and the cracked headlight. He mumbled to himself in both disgust and surprise and then he saw the little girl sitting between Keal and some woman as the car stopped in front of him. Keal got out and Burdean met him at the front of the car and cracked him right in the nose. Keal's knees buckled and he backpedaled and then landed smackflat on his ass. The blood spit from his nostril and he winced and squeezed his eyes shut and he opened them to see Burdean coming on. He reached down and grabbed Keal by the collar of his coat and he raised him to his feet and then he hit him again, a hard fist against his forehead and Keal staggered back but stayed upright and he started moving around the side of the car to get away from him.

"Damn it," he said and he wiped the blood from his nose as he moved to put the car between them. "We got enough to contend with."

"Disappear on me one more time."

Burdean stalked him. The men shuffling around the car. Keal trying to explain and Burdean interrupting him with promises of what he was about to do to him and when they had made a full circle around the car, Cara and the girl climbed out and Cara held her hand and they started walking down the sidewalk. It stopped both men from what they were doing.

"Where the hell do you think you're going?" Burdean said.

They kept walking.

"Hey. Hey!"

"Play your stupid game," Cara said.

Keal held his nose pinched between his fingers and he hurried over to Cara and the girl and said I told you when we got here that I'd try to explain.

"You're not trying to explain anything as far as I can see."

Burdean came around the car and met them on the sidewalk and said I don't know who you are or where you came from but that girl ain't going nowhere. You don't know nothing about nothing.

"I know when I see a kid running down a road being chased by a man she don't know that something is bad wrong."

"What are you talking about?"

"Can we all hold on a damn second?" Keal said. He sniffed and spit and his nose had just about stopped bleeding.

"What did you do?" Burdean asked him.

"Me and her went back out to the church."

"For what?"

"To look around."

Burdean grabbed Keal by the arm and dragged him away from Cara and the girl. He leaned into Keal and he raised a fist and held it under Keal's chin and said in a growl don't you ever slip out on me again. You hear me? Goddamn it that's twice. We are in this shit together. I brought you on a job and not the other way around and I don't know what we've ended up in but if you make one more decision on your own without squaring it with me then your life will not end up the way you want it to. He let go of his arm and shoved him.

"Fair to say it already has."

"I don't care about your life one way or another. Are you listening to what I'm telling you? This shit is serious."

"I know it's serious."

"Then act like it."

"I will."

"Then tell me who that woman is and what happened."

Keal recounted it all. The bodies sat upright and then going back down into the cellar to look into the room and hearing the car horn and finding the girl with the doors locked and the men trying to get to her. And the guns coming out and the chase down the road and hitting a yellow car with the big car when he was trying to catch up to the girl and the woman had to jump in with them.

"This is becoming a thing."

"What else was I supposed to do? I ain't actually versed in this kind of shit."

"And them other two that showed up. They're dead?"

"One was laying in the road. She hit him with her car. The other one I thought was dead but turns out he wasn't. But I'm pretty sure he is now."

"They have a phone?"

"I didn't ask."

"They saw the car."

Keal nodded. Burdean pulled out a cigarette and Keal took one.

"You didn't call anybody. Did you?" Keal asked.

"No and I turned it off. Even though I'm sure my damn phone at home is ringing off the hook. I don't guess I can go back there ever."

Cara walked over to the men and interrupted them.

"She told me she's hungry," she said.

"She told you?" Burdean said.

"With words?" Keal said.

"What is wrong with you two?"

"We can't get her to talk," Keal said.

"She said she's hungry and she said to tell you she speaks English."

The men glanced over at the girl. She looked tired. Heavy eyes grown darker in recent minutes. Like the fade of a sunset. In her hands she held the crucifix from around Cara's neck and she seemed both rigid and fragile. As if she had not quite decided which to be.

"How old do you think she is?" Burdean said.

"She said she's nine."

"You asked her?"

"Have either of you ever had a conversation with another person before?"

"I told you she won't talk to us."

Burdean took out a lighter and lit the cigarettes. Cara held out her hand and he gave her one.

"Now it's your turn," Cara said.

"For what?"

"I'm about thirty seconds from taking her to some form of law unless you can convince me otherwise. And you got your own thirty seconds to do that because to say that I'm scared to death right now would shortchange it. I could probably say the same for her."

The three of them stood there smoking and Burdean kept it concise. We had a job to do and we went to do it and didn't know exactly what we were supposed to be finding. We found that little girl down in the cellar and we weren't the only ones sent looking because there was a bunch of dead men laying around when we got there. So we don't know who brought her there or why and we didn't exactly have no choice but to take her with us. Like you apparently.

"It started before that," Keal said.

Burdean cut his eyes at him. Drew on the cigarette.

"Might as well tell it," he said.

Keal asked her if she lived somewhere out there or if she

just happened to be cutting through the county. She said she lived a few miles and some winding roads away from the church but she never liked to drive by it and she was only killing time and trying not to think when she ended up on the church road. They smoked for a minute as if letting it all catch up with them and the girl had sat down on the curb. A couple of teenagers came out of the pawn shop, one carrying a banjo and the other carrying a crossbow and when Burdean didn't think they were walking fast enough past them he told them to mind their own business. The boys were confused by his bark but kept moving. Finally Keal looked at Cara and asked her if she knew anything about the abandoned church.

"Yeah. I told you. I avoid it. It creeps me out."

"And what about the woods?"

"What does that mean?" she asked.

"There's nothing in those woods," Burdean said.

"You changed your tune."

"Some sleep and a pack of cigarettes will do that."

"What are y'all talking about?"

Cara waited on them but they went silent. The men looked at each other. Looked over at the girl whose head was now resting on her folded arms on top of her knees. They looked over at the hotel that time forgot and up and down the tracks and around the meager streets. She didn't know why she wasn't walking away from them. Why she wasn't going home or going back to work or catching a ride to get her Volkswagen or going anywhere besides here. She was about to tell them that she had no choice and you can fight me if you want to but I'm calling the police and figuring out where this little girl belongs. The words were forming in her mouth when Keal spoke.

"Even before we got into all that other stuff the whole night was strange."

"Strange," she said.

Keal nodded. He tossed his cigarette and then he glanced at Burdean, waiting on Burdean to stop him but Burdean remained quiet and Keal said it all started with this old woman wandering through the dark.

Cara pushed up the sleeves of her sweatshirt as if getting ready for some task and her eyes moved between the men. The older one with the white in his beard and the ridges around his eyes and the younger one with the look of the lost and the lazy curl in the length of his hair and the age that seemed to be rushing on him at this very minute. She thought of waking during the night and the feeling that something was going on with the old woman and she flushed, knowing now that she had been right in ways she did not even understand. That whatever it was that had spoken to her was real.

The sensation made her suspect the men and their possession of the child both more and less and before she could decide which side to fall on, the sirens began to sound from somewhere beyond the grotesque little town. The faint yowls like spirits calling, a requiem for the day to come. Their heads turned. Listening. Knowing that the things they had seen and decisions they had made could no longer be held inside a room of their own.

20

Roadblocks had been set up at the church and on the other end of the road where the sedan had come to a stop. At the church end there was a gathering of volunteer deputies and firemen and emergency medics and others whose job it was to show up for carnage. But they had been told to wait right where they were until further instructed and the crew stood around with their arms folded, talking about wives and deerhunting and football and comparing whatever they had all done the weekend before.

Two men moved alone between the roadblocks. A county investigator wearing a tie that was a little too short and a navy windbreaker with his badge pinned on his belt. The other man did not wear a badge. He did not wear a uniform. He wore a long and welltraveled leather coat with a fur collar and a watch chain hung from a coat pocket. His cheeks were pocked with scars and his hair fell long and slick. Bloodshot eyes. His expression stuck in a dirty grin.

Before anyone was let into the scene the man in the leather coat strolled around the churchyard. He studied the faces of the deceased and he looked inside the van and truck. He took a flashlight from the county investigator and stepped down into the cellar. He went into the room at its end and touched his fingers to the drawings on the wall and then he pulled a piece of chalk from his pocket and added a lightning bolt. When he was done in the cellar he walked the church road in the direction that they had run. The county investigator rolled along behind him in his government car with the brake lights glowing red as the man walked without haste, as if enjoying the stroll through the macabre. The sun fell closer to the horizon and the rim of the sky turned to fire, ablaze in orange and gold as the hardwood shadows fell across the road and the man loped along with one hand in his pocket and the other twirling the watch chain. He stopped at the broken man that Cara had hit, his eyes frozen open as if gathering a final impression of a sky he never wanted to forget and then the man walked to the Volkswagen and opened the door and leaned his head in and picked through the clothes on the backseat and the fastfood bags on the floorboard. He found an insurance card in the glovebox and took note of the address and then he got into the car with the county investigator. They drove the snaking road a few miles further to where the sedan had drifted off into the brush. The man in the leather coat got out alone. The engine was still running with the driver slumped over the wheel and his shirt and pants wet with blood. The man reached in the window and took the driver by the hair and lifted his head back and looked at his openmouthed face and then he let go and the driver's forehead thumped against the steering wheel.

Back at the church the volunteers and coroner and medics and tow truck driver waited while the two men sat down in the car, the man in the leather coat talking to the investigator without looking at him and then the investigator jotting down a note. A thick envelope changed hands and then the investigator climbed out. He called them over and they gathered around. The man in the leather coat waited in the car. The county investigator then told them what to do. Pile all the bodies onto the back of a truck and close the cellar doors and then tow away all the vehicles to wherever you want to tow them. All except for that yellow one. Take it back to where it belongs. The investigator then handed the note to a tow truck driver and on it was written Cara's address and what to put in the trunk before he left her vehicle there.

EVENING

21

They got off the street. Burdean shot pool downstairs and smoked cigarette after cigarette. Cara and the girl went into the room upstairs while Keal went to find them something to eat.

He discovered a place two blocks away with a chalkboard sidewalk sign that read CHILI DOGS AND ICE CREAM. He pulled open the glass door and walked inside. The floor was checkerboard tile and there was a bookshelf filled with paperbacks against the wall with potted plants sitting on top of it. Five kids sat crammed around a table and two mothers sat at another and when one of the kids called for mom, one of the mothers said we told you to just eat it. There was a counter in the rear with a coffee machine and stacks of napkins and next to the counter a woman with glasses on the end of her nose sat on a stool counting the cash in the register. She looked up and saw Keal approaching and she closed the register drawer and held up her hand.

"Before we get started we don't have any ice cream," she said.

"They sure as hell don't," one of the kids shouted.

"Hush," a mother said.

He didn't want ice cream but for some reason he now wanted to know why it was on the sidewalk sign if they didn't have any. So he asked.

"Same reason as everybody is out of everything," the woman said. "Can't get no supplier to fill an order and if I could then I can't get no truck to bother stopping through here. Not but about once a damn month. I could get some shitty ice cream but don't nobody want shitty ice cream. You'd think we were somewhere on the other side of the world."

"You could still take it off the sign."

"Call it optimism."

"You got chili dogs?"

"I got dogs. No chili."

"You got buns to put the dogs in?"

"Now you're being ridiculous," she said. "How many you want?"

Before he could answer there was a commotion behind him as the two mothers got up from their table and got the five kids up from the other and they all shuffled out of the door pushing and pulling and grunting at one another.

"Thank the dear Lord," the woman said.

"Let me get four dogs."

"Four."

"No. Five. I should get an extra."

"An extra?"

Keal nodded and she seemed to be waiting for him to say

something else but he didn't. She wore a bandana tied around her neck and she raised it and wiped at the side of her mouth before she stood from the stool and went through a swinging door behind the counter. Keal moved to a rack of potato chips at the end of the counter and he grabbed four bags and set them next to the register and then the woman came back through the door.

"It's you," she said. "Ain't it?"

He moved his head in a quick shake.

"Keal. Raylene's boy."

"Yeah?"

"That you?"

"It is."

She came from around the counter and she reached out and hugged him around the waist. He halfhugged her back and then she reached up and patted his cheek.

"You're about as handsome as ever."

"I don't think I was ever handsome."

"That ain't what Raylene would say. She thought you were the most handsome child ever born and would just about fight anybody who argued with her."

She moved back around the counter and stood smiling at Keal. She was a short woman with short hair and a few freckles across her nose. He tried to place her but he couldn't and then she said I used to work with Raylene at the grocery store. Can't remember which one but one of them. You were probably ten years old or so. You'd come in the store and steal gum when you didn't think nobody was looking but we were looking. Raylene said you used to try and get away with a lot of stuff but she always knew. Just didn't want to embarrass you by calling you out. I remember I'd whoop mine if I caught them doing just about anything Jesus wouldn't do and she said if you did that you'd spend all your time whooping. That's how she was. She rolled along when most of us were busy worrying over every other minute of the day. But not Raylene. She just pushed her sleeves up and kept going. My Lord that was twentysomething years ago. You still got some of that boy in your eyes or else I don't think I'd known you. My Lord. I'm talking too much. That was four dogs plus an extra. That what it was?

"That's it," Keal said.

"Let me fix you up. Get some coffee right there. It's on the house if you can stand to drink it. I like to give it some gusto myself."

She whirled around and slipped back through the swinging door.

Keal picked up a white cup and poured the coffee. And she was right. It had some gusto and he could only manage a few sips. He moved to the door and opened it and tossed the coffee out and he stood there in the open doorway remembering the grocery store and his mother with her hair in a ponytail and the green apron she had to wear as she ran the register or sacked groceries or swept the floor or did whatever else she was asked to do. He then stepped back inside. He tossed away the cup and waited at the counter. Bumps and knocks came from behind the swinging door and then the woman reappeared carrying a brown paper bag filled with the order.

"You still live in your momma's trailer?"

"Yeah. But I had it moved."

"How come?"

"Just didn't like that spot out there anymore."

"What do you do now?"

"Ma'am?"

"What do you do for work?"

"I don't know. Same as most people. Patch it together as good as I can."

She studied him a minute. Set the bag on the counter. She changed from an old friend of his mother's into a mother herself.

"That don't sound like an answer, Keal."

"It is."

"Too many people around here give those kind of answers. This ain't the land of opportunity but there's more to do than patch it together. I know what it means when people say things like that."

She pushed the bag toward him. Then she took another from beneath the counter and she dropped a stack of napkins and mustard and ketchup packets and the bags of chips inside.

"Sounds to me like you're still doing it," she said.

"Doing what?"

"Trying to get away with stuff when you don't think nobody is looking."

Keal picked up the bags.

"Maybe I am. And you know what else. Maybe I have to."

He then asked her how much and she told him. He dropped some money on the counter and he went out the door. He stopped at the sidewalk sign and he looked back inside. She was still watching him from behind the counter. He then reached inside the bag and pulled out a napkin and he wiped ICE CREAM from the sign and he walked on.

22

When Keal returned with the food Cara and the girl came downstairs. Burdean said he wasn't hungry but the rest of them ate the hot dogs and chips quickly and with big bites. When they were finished Cara took the girl back to the room and then rejoined the men.

The three of them stood next to one of the grand old hotel windows. Several of the panes cracked and patched with duct tape that gave the appearance of the crooked trails of some map. They exchanged everything but names. Burdean wouldn't let them. Keal explained the old woman appearing from the trees while they were sitting around the fire, killing time and waiting to return to the church. Cara listened with intent about the wandering of the old woman and then she told them her name was Wanetah and I have been watching her fade for a while. She didn't know where she was, I don't understand how she could have ended up in the cellar with the child.

"There is a whole lot of shit that nobody understands," Keal said.

Burdean listened silently. The door jingled with locals coming in and buying and selling at the pawn shop counter and they would hush until the room was empty again. A burly man with a braided beard and leather vest made the deals and went about his business and acted as if the three of them were not there. As if it had been part of the package that Burdean made when he brokered the room upstairs. You do not see me or anyone I'm with. Ever.

The day fell fast. Keal rubbed at his eyes and Burdean asked him when was the last time he slept and he shrugged his shoulders. The burly man shuffled around the pool table, pulling chains of the neon lights that hung on walls and in windows. The lights clicked and buzzed and then warmed into yellows and reds and blues and gave the twilight an electrical glow.

"You don't sleep?" Cara said.

"Not like normal people."

"What's a normal people?"

He shook his head. She moved to the pawn shop counter and asked the burly man for a beer and he reached into a standing cooler and handed her a bottle. Then she said I'm going to check on the girl.

"Hold on," Burdean said. "She'll talk to you. Right?"

"She did before."

"I figure the only way out of this is to get her to give us some answers. Can you?"

She drank from the beer. Glanced at Keal.

"I agree," he said.

"I can try. If you really think she has any."

105

She walked out and around the side of the building and they could hear her steps as she climbed the metal grate stairway. The burly man disappeared down a hallway and a door opened and closed.

Burdean picked up the nine-ball from the pool table and tossed it between his hands. And then he said I tell you what we should do right now and that's get in the car and start driving and don't stop until me and you both are about three states away.

"Just run off and leave them."

"Hell yes. Run off and leave them. Don't neither one of them mean shit to me."

"If we were gonna run off and leave them then we never should have brought them with us."

"I didn't bring them with us. I brought that kid with us. You did the rest. If you could have just sat here like we agreed to then there wouldn't be an extra. It ain't like she can't just go home anyway."

"It's too late for that now."

"No it ain't. The car is right out there and the keys are right in my pocket."

"They're in my pocket," Keal said. "Besides you know when the law gets out there they'll see her car and then go right to her house."

"She don't know our names and other than that we were only seen by dead men."

"We found that little girl in a cellar, Burdean. Where those dead men lay."

"And we got her out. She's alive. She ain't my problem. I say we let whatever-her-name-is take it from here and we hit the damn road."

"I ain't leaving."

Burdean tossed the nine-ball on the pool table and it landed in a knock.

"We'll see how long that lasts. My clock is ticking."

There was a table and chairs by one of the tall windows and Keal plopped down.

"You need to go lay down," Burdean said. "I don't see how you do that shit."

"It's not by choice. Mostly."

"People got to sleep."

"If I go to sleep now I'm gonna wake up and you'll be gone and then what."

"That's exactly how I felt when I woke up to find that you'd hightailed it."

Burdean moved behind the counter and took two beers from the cooler. He returned to Keal and set them on the table. Keal stared out the window, his eyes rimmed in gray. Burdean sat and took a long drink from the beer. And then another long drink and it was gone. Keal hadn't moved. He sat sunkeyed as if under the spell of some charlatan. Burdean set down his empty and then picked up the beer he brought over for Keal. He looked at him and imagined them being other men in another place where there was warm weather and a deck to sit on and there could be more beer brought over by a waitress with pigtails and maybe some women would come out on the deck and join them and they could drink and watch the day turn to night and then maybe a band would show up and play and maybe they could get a couple of the women to dance with them and they could all have a drunken and careless night and the burden of a hang-over and the morning clarity of what everyone really looked like would be the only consequences. He felt like he had done such things and he tried to remember where and when and with who but as he sat there he could not conjure the faces or the joy of such nights and he wondered if these were the memories of some other man.

Outside the world was turning blue.

"Maybe I should tell you something," Burdean said.

Keal turned to Burdean, his head leaned to the side. The tilt of exhaustion.

"I won't call to see what the hell is going on because I don't know who we're doing this for."

Keal's head straightened. He reached and took the beer from Burdean.

"You said it was the same guy as always."

"Well. I lied."

Burdean stood and took off his coat and draped it across the back of the chair and he sat back down. He pulled the cigarette pack from the pocket of his flannel shirt and dropped it between them.

"My phone rang and I answered it. This man said he had a job for me. Said he was given my name and I said okay. I just figured it was another 'go get this guy who owes me some money' or 'meet somebody at a gas station and hand off a duffel bag.' Same kind of shit me and you usually do."

"Who was it?"

"I don't know who it was. That's the point."

"Then why'd you say yes?"

"Because he told me he'd give me four times what I usually get if I didn't ask no questions. So I didn't ask no questions. Godalmighty. I knew better than to do that shit."

"I appreciate you dragging me along. I don't really like getting shot at. Or doing the shooting. I never done that before and don't plan on doing it again."

"If I was you I wouldn't get in the habit of deciding what you will or won't do before it happens."

They both tapped out a cigarette. They both lit theirs. They both stared out at the empty street.

"So?" Keal said. "Why do you think it matters?"

Burdean took a drag and ashed the cigarette in the empty bottle.

"It matters because there is no face on this thing. So how are we supposed to know who or what we're looking for? Or who or what to stay away from? Even though at the end of the day there is really only one answer we need to wash our hands of all this."

"What answer is that?"

"What to do with the girl."

Keal stood from the chair and moved over to the window and outside the sky had changed again. A wall of stonegray clouds had formed in the southern sky and carried the look of menace. Sucking away the evening light. A new wind pushed leaves and trash along the street.

"They say this is going to be the worst year yet," Keal said.

"Worst year yet for what?"

"The storms."

"They say that every year."

"They been right lately."

"Good," Burdean said. "Maybe one will blow up here in the next couple of hours and carry us all away to the promised land. Wherever that is."

"Probably be less people around here next year than it is now. Seems that's how it's been going."

"I like it better that way."

"You might run out of things to do. People to do them with."

"Not in my business. Vice doesn't need much of a population."

Keal turned from the window and he walked over and sat down again.

"There's one other bit I should probably tell you," Burdean said. "The last thing he said."

He smoked again. Extending the moment as if he didn't want to explain.

Keal waited. He had never known Burdean to be anything other than a picture of certainty as they traversed the night and did whatever clandestine task they were being paid to do. But he had changed in this moment, the smoke and the neon and the dusty edge of night wrapping him in doubt.

Burdean dropped the butt into the bottle and raised his eyes to Keal and said I wish he wouldn't have said it but he said it and I blew it off for the most part until we started to get deeper into the things we got into last night. I thought about it when we first went to the church and saw the light we didn't expect to see and I thought about it when the old woman showed up out of absolute nowhere and I thought about it when those shotguns fired off in the night. Ever since it's all I been thinking about. I got the instructions and was about to hang up the phone when he said my name. I waited for him to say something else but all he did was say my name again. And then silence. It felt like he was playing with me, seeing how long I'd hold on. And then he told me this last thing and I swear on my life it was in some kind of different voice, like all of a sudden he was at the bottom of a hole. Deep. Empty.

Keal shifted in his chair. Leaned forward some. Burdean took a quick look around the empty room as if maybe someone was watching or listening and then he repeated to Keal the last thing the voice had said. The truth about the world is that everything is possible and you are a part of that now. You have become a part of the hand of God. And the hand of God is soaked in blood.

Burdean's eyes returned to the window. There was the coming night. Keal stood up. He began walking around the pool table. One lap and then another with his mind spinning and he was about to tell Burdean that he was right. Let's get in the car and go because I don't know how to deal with this and I don't know how to deal with dreaming about that old woman and then having her show up in the woods as if she walked right out of my head and thinking she was somehow my mother and I don't know how to deal with the dream about the lightning and the thunder and the flames that I haven't even told you about and then waking up to find the little girl with her fists balled up and her face red and staring at the sky like her eyes could rip right through it and if the hand of God is soaked in blood then I don't want to be a part of that any more than you do. Burdean fiddled with the cigarette pack and Keal made laps around the pool table and he was figuring out how to deal with the guilt of running away and how he would ever stop thinking about leaving the girl and the woman no matter how old he lived to be and he was getting ready to tell Burdean let's make a run for it when the door jingled and opened and Cara and the child stood there.

23

Cara crossed the room and stood next to Keal at the pool table. Then she leaned close to him and spoke in a quiet voice.

"She won't talk to me here but she said she would talk to me at my house."

"Your house?"

"Speak up," Burdean said.

"I told him she said she would tell me more if we went to my house."

"How does she know about your house?" Burdean said.

"Because I told her I have a house which I don't suppose is any big news. And she said she wanted to go there, that she wasn't going to talk in this place."

"Why not?"

"Why don't you ask her?"

Burdean slumped down in his chair. Laid his head back

and said something to himself that they couldn't hear. He then looked at the girl and she pointed out the window and to the big car.

"That ain't a good idea," Keal said.

"You wanted answers," Cara said. "If she's acting like she'll give some at my place then that's how you'll get them. Let's do what she asks us to do and see."

Burdean pulled himself up from the chair and stood. He walked over to the girl.

"How come you can't talk to her here?"

The girl walked past him and over to the pool table and she pushed the cue ball around.

"That's what I figured," he said.

"It's almost dark," Keal said. "We could probably go out there now."

"And what if we can't?"

"Then we'll just drive right by and keep going," Cara said.

Burdean studied her. Suspecting her of something he couldn't quite name but realizing she had risked to become a part of this. Her willingness to remain somehow aggravated him.

"I guess we could always go to your house," she said. A smart little smile across her face.

Burdean shook his head.

"Or yours," she said to Keal.

"I don't have a house. I have a trailer."

"For chrissake," Burdean said. "Just get in the damn car and let's go."

24

As they drove, Burdean began to try and put the voice with a face. Any face. Someone he had overlooked or some clue he had missed and he found himself returning to a sultry night in a swampy bar. Over a year ago at least, he thought. Plenty of time for someone to be forgotten if that's what they wanted.

The bar was a ramshackle structure, patched together with rusted sheet metal and plywood. It was hidden way back in the dark, along a strip of river vein. A dirt road that wasn't on any map leading to it. A spotlight hung from a post and cast light across the slowflowing water, where fishing boats were tied to a pier with bowed planks and bugs the size of small birds swarmed and smacked against the spotlight bulb like little hellbent kamikazes. Inside the bar was lit with the orangey glow of kerosene lamps parceled out among the few tables and set upon shelves hammered randomly into the wall and there were only two things to drink. Tequila or beer. And nobody cared. It was the perfect place for not wanting to be found.

On the night Burdean was thinking of he had just left his house and a woman he had been holed up with for two days and two nights and they had done nothing but drink screwtop wine and smoke cigarettes and tear at one another and he needed to be somewhere else for a little while. He had been sitting at the end of the bar, tapping his finger on the bottom of a kerosene lamp and watching the shadow of his beer can dance in the wave of the light, trying to decide if he wanted her to sneak away or if he was hoping she was readying herself for another round. He wasn't sure and he was going to be satisfied with whatever she decided. He was raising his hand to motion to the bartender, who sat on a stool in the corner picking at the skin of her wrinkled hand, when the screen door spring wrenched and then the door slapped shut as two men walked in and sat down as far away from Burdean as they could sit. Which wasn't far. He only glanced over his shoulder and took little notice of the men and then he called to the bartender and she gave him another shot and another beer and then she carried beers to the men who had just sat down.

Four teenagers were the only others in the room. Two boys and two girls and their chatter and the guitar twang coming from a radio sounded against the multitude of croaks that swelled across the night. Burdean took his phone from his pocket and set it on the bar and he wanted her to call and didn't want her to call. He looked at his watch and he had been gone for almost two hours and he figured that she had gathered whatever she had brought with her and maybe even some of his things and slipped away.

He put his phone back into his pocket. He lit a cigarette and sipped from his beer and thought of the smooth skin of the woman's back and he imagined her naked across his bed. Lying on her stomach. Waiting for him to come back. He had always found pleasure in the solitude that followed such encounters but in that moment as he sat there alone at what could have been the end of the world he had been filled with the strange sensation that something inside of him was at risk. As if he could walk outside and stand on the end of the pier and see pieces of himself floating by in the muddy water and he took a long swig of beer to rid himself of the sentiment and when he sat his bottle back down on the bar, a finger tapped him on the shoulder.

He turned and looked at Hoss. A seasoned nightcrawler like himself. His mouth worked a wad of gum beneath a bushy mustache and he wore a t-shirt with the sleeves cut off. His arms were dotted with oddshaped hearts and stars and other undefinable objects, the result of tattoos he had given himself because he had never seen the reason in giving anyone any money for a job he believed he was perfectly capable of doing.

"Hey," he said.

"Hey yourself."

He sat down next to Burdean.

"I ain't got long," he said.

Burdean gave him a puzzled look.

"So listen," Hoss said.

"Hey Burdean. How ya doing? I'm fine, Hoss. How about you? That's usually how this goes."

"This ain't usual."

Burdean sighed. Drank. Smoked.

"Just go back over there," he said.

116

"Listen," Hoss said.

"Quit saying that."

"If there was a job, something bigger. Could you do it?"

"Bigger how?"

Hoss turned his head and glanced back at the man he had left at the table.

"He didn't say."

"Who didn't say?"

He pointed. Burdean looked around at the man who had come in with Hoss. He had moved the kerosene lamp right in front of his face and he sat with a sinister stillness and stared at the men. The flame of the lamp reflected in his round spectacles. Long sideburns ran the length of his cheeks and he sat with his hands folded on the table. There was an agelessness about the man and his features that held Burdean's attention for a moment before he turned back to Hoss.

"What kind of job?"

"He didn't say."

"Why can't he come over here?" Burdean said.

"He didn't say that either."

"What the fuck did he say?"

"He said if there was something bigger could you do it."

"Why don't you do it?"

"He didn't ask me to."

"How come?"

"He said this was something for you."

"He don't know me."

"He must. Somehow."

"He said my name?"

Hoss nodded. He reached over and drank from Burdean's

beer and then he ran his eyes around the bar as if anticipating some ambush.

"What's wrong with you?" Burdean said.

"Look. He asked me if I knew where to find you and I said you come in here sometimes."

"How many times you and him been in here looking?"

"One. Tonight."

Burdean drank.

"Is that luck or you following me? Because if you been following me then you been by my house and I've told you about that."

"I got better shit to do than follow you around."

"How come you helping him track me down?"

"Same as always. A few dollars. He's looking to hire you, Burdean. He ain't looking to kill you. I don't think."

"Funny."

Burdean finished his cigarette and dropped it into an empty beer can.

"I can do whatever. Just give him my damn number."

"I already did. He said he wanted to lay eyes on you before he called you."

"What the hell does that mean?"

"I don't know. I guess he heard how pretty you are."

Burdean then took out his phone again and waved it at the man. Pursed his lips and shook his head in unmistakable disgust at the theatrics of the exchange.

"Tell him if he ain't got the balls to walk over here and sit down and buy me a drink like a good hire would do then don't bother."

"I ain't telling him nothing."

"Why not?"

"I ain't sure. I just don't like him. He makes me feel funny."

"Funny how?"

"Just funny. Like when you get off a roller coaster and your guts ain't quite settled."

"I ain't worried about that. Roller coasters don't bother me none."

"Then you ain't got nothing to worry about."

"That's what I said."

They were interrupted by the slapping of the screen door closing. They both looked at the table and the man was gone.

"Hope he wasn't your ride," Burdean said.

The bartender brought Burdean another beer and another shot without him asking and then his phone rang. He answered it and the woman was still at his house and still ready and she told him to come on back. We're not done. He hung up and he shot the tequila. He took a drink of beer to wash it down and then he handed the beer to Hoss and told him he could have the rest.

"What if he was?" Hoss said.

"Was what?"

"My ride."

Burdean shrugged and then he stood up and laid cash on the bar. He slapped Hoss on the shoulder and said I can't help you. I got needs to attend to. And one more thing. You tell that creepy son of a bitch if I ever see him again I'll wring his damn neck.

Burdean had seen him once more. Or he thought he had

seen him. A couple of weeks later. He had been drinking a midday beer in the pawn shop, hiding out in his room upstairs for a few days after delivering a trunkload of suitcases packed with he didn't know what to a trio of Mexicans waiting for him in the parking lot at the Mississippi Welcome Center at the foot of the big river bridge in Vicksburg. He had walked over to the pool table and was about to put two quarters in the slot when he looked out of the window and the man was standing on the sidewalk, leaned against a lamppost. The same sideburns and the same spectacles and the same stare. He wore a denim shirt buttoned to the neck. Burdean stared back at him through the window and the night in the lamplit bar flashed across his mind. In the daylight the man was different. He had the look of an oldtime preacher. Or maybe a serial killer. And when it was evident the man was not going to look away, Burdean did and he dropped the quarters in the slot and the pool balls tumbled free. He racked the balls and then after the clatter of the break Burdean looked back up and the man was gone.

He set his beer down on the edge of the pool table and he walked out and looked up and down the sidewalk and then he walked across the street and across the railroad tracks and he kept looking. He passed the yellowbrick post office and he passed by a welltanned roofing crew standing around a sandwich truck and he stuck his head inside a sparsely stocked used record store and he tried to tell himself he had imagined it. That it could not have been the same man. But he kept going. He sat down at the counter of a café and had a cup of coffee and sipped it slowly and cut his eyes out of the café window, believing if he was there long enough the man would appear again on the sidewalk. He had to tell the cook at the flatiron grill twice he didn't want any lunch and then when he was finished with the coffee he walked out and stood at the store window of a quilt maker where a woman with a puffy bun of gray hair tied up on her head sat at a sewing machine and worked patches onto a quilt. He pretended to watch her while instead he studied the reflection of the window for the man. The woman paused and waved at Burdean and caught his attention and he waved back and then he walked around the corner and leaned against the brick wall of the building and lit a cigarette and cussed.

When he returned to the flophouse he moved up the metal grate staircase with heavy feet, trying to make as much noise as he could. Trying to sound the alarm that he was coming because he had the suspicion that the man was waiting for him in his room. When he got to the top of the stairs he opened the hallway door and slammed it behind him and then he walked with the same heavy steps along the corridor. His boots hard against the wood floor. He could not remember if he had locked the padlock and when he got to his room the lock was not closed and he lifted it from the padlock and held it inside his fist to make his fist heavier and he pushed open the door but there was nothing and nobody. He stayed at the flophouse a few extra days. Waiting and hoping the man would reappear but he did not. He called Hoss to see if Hoss had seen or heard from the man again and Hoss said hell no and I hope I don't never see him.

Now as Burdean drove, all he could hear was the voice as it sunk into its declarations of God and blood and he grew hot in frustration at his own mistake of not finding out who he was talking to and what exactly was expected of him. The mistakes of a much younger man. All because of money. The big car moved through the hills and in the mirror he peeked at the woman and the girl in the backseat and then he glanced over at Keal and as the voice sounded in his head he could only imagine it coming from the thin mouth of the thin face framed by the sideburns.

NIGHTFALL

25

Cara's house was boxlike and woodframed. The limbs of a pecan tree hung over the roof that dropped pecans in random knocks during the season like bits of summer hail. She had killed the springtime painting the small house a fresh coat of white and she painted each of the shutters a different color. Colors her grandmother would have liked and she wished she had painted the house years earlier before her grandmother had passed. Pastel shades of red, blue, green, and orange and in the headlights of the big car the house had the flair of a candied treat.

A short and rutted driveway ran along the side of the house and the Volkswagen had been delivered there as if it had never left. They debated the message in this and sat staring. During the drive the girl had laid her head across Cara's lap in the backseat and she was still resting there. Finally Cara said there's a good chance that the tow truck driver knows that's my car and did me a favor bringing it here instead of the lot. It's a small place you know.

"That's too easy," Burdean said. "Cars that hit people and leave them dead in the road don't get towed back to their owners."

"It could also be true," she said.

"Is your front door open?"

"I don't remember locking it."

"Did you leave those lights on?"

"I always leave lights on."

Burdean tapped his fingers on the steering wheel. Flipped the headlights on bright and the beams spread around the width of the house and stretched into the dark behind it. Then he reached into his coat and took out his pistol and told them to wait there. I'll be right back unless there is something in there that has a different idea. He then turned to Keal and said get over here behind the wheel and roll down the window and if you hear anything that makes you think you should take off then take off. Both men got out of the car and passed in the headlights and Keal got behind the wheel. Burdean paused in the beams for a moment. His figure splitting the light. His shadow stretched against the house. When Keal closed the car door and rolled down the window the girl sat up in the backseat so she could see.

Burdean crossed the yard to the front door. He pulled open the screen and stood there listening. Then he turned the door handle and pushed the door open. He stood in the wash of house light and waited, his pistol raised. Then he stepped inside. There were only four rooms and a kitchen that sat lopsided on a badly done enclosure of a side porch. They could see Burdean move through the house through the open curtains.

"Why do you think he said it like that?" Cara said.

"Said what?"

"He said I'll be right back unless there is something in there. Not someone. Something."

The girl raised the framed angel and pointed at it and then pointed at the house.

"What does that mean?" Keal said.

"Is there an angel in here?" Cara asked.

"God I hope. It sure ain't him."

The girl then raised her finger and drew something in the air that neither of them understood and then she lowered her eyes again to the drawing.

Keal shook his head. Moved in the seat. Dropped his hand over the steering wheel as if they were cruising.

"Well?" Cara said.

"Well."

"Why do you think he said it like that?"

"I don't know. A manner of speaking, I suppose."

"A manner of speaking."

"Don't make a big deal out of it."

"Pretend like you're not thinking the same way if you want."

They watched Burdean open closets. Look around and beneath the sparse furniture and behind doors. And then he disappeared from view as he shifted to the back of the house.

"There's an attic," Cara said.

"Where's the pull?" Keal said.

"Hallway."

"He'll find it. Although that ain't the best place to hide if you're looking to waylay somebody."

"How would you know?"

He looked over his shoulder at Cara. The child shrugged and Keal turned his attention back to Burdean. A possum appeared from somewhere beneath the jungle of azaleas surrounding the house that grew wild and shapeless. Keal leaned his head out of the open window. Croaks and chirps chanted in the night and a low moon hung in a starbrushed sky.

Burdean then appeared in the opening of the front door. A figure of indecision, looking back inside and then looking out into the night and looking up and down the empty road. He pushed open the screen and stepped out into the yard and stuck the pistol into the back of his pants. He lit a cigarette and stood there smoking, covered in the white light of the beams. Keal started to open the car door but Burdean raised his hand to hold him there, turned his head as if he had heard something and then he spotted the possum rustling through the azaleas. He pulled the pistol and pointed at the pinktailed creature and cocked the hammer. Cara yelled out of the window. Don't you do it. He lowered the pistol and returned it to his pants and then he grudgingly waved for them to come on.

26

Keal and Burdean stood in the front room. There was a sofa covered by a quilt and a television in the corner on a short bookshelf with no books. Only a candle on one shelf and nothing else. No rug on the floor. Another room had a small round table and two mismatched chairs. Empty wine bottles sat on the table and a box was on the floor with wine necks sticking out. In another room there was a bed that had been broken down and the headboard and rails and mattress leaned against the wall and a chest of drawers was against the wall with the drawers missing and an empty picture frame lay on top.

Cara and the girl were behind the closed door of her bedroom.

Each wall of the house was painted the same pale yellow. There were no photographs, no clocks, nothing on the walls, no semblance of any memory or past and no notion of what Cara liked or admired or preferred. The house seemed to have been sanitized from the workings of life. The only thing that hung on the wall was the crucifix which the girl had draped on a nail that was in the wall next to the telephone where Cara had once upon a time kept a calendar. The two men milled from room to room waiting on Cara to emerge from the bedroom with any kind of information from the girl, footfalls and creaks as they paced and cigarette smoke filling the rooms and Burdean with his hand on the pistol even though they had lapped the house several times and it seemed to satisfy their need for refuge. Keal kept asking. What do you think is going on? Burdean kept shrugging and pacing. Burdean made one more lap through the rooms and leaned his ear against the bedroom door and when he heard no voices he huffed and walked outside.

Keal went into the bathroom and he was struck by its contradiction to the rest of the house. The built-in shelf was crammed with towels and a couple of wadded robes and t-shirts and underwear and the bottom shelf was littered with paint trays and brushes and the leftover cans of color she had used to paint the house shutters. The tub was lined with bottles of shampoo and conditioner and razors both new and old were stacked into a plastic cup that sat on a rack that hung on the showerhead. Wet and faded washrags gathered in the rack in soggy clumps. Everything needed cleaning and it seemed as if he had walked into a different house, the personality of the bathroom standing alone in its clutter and grime as if in opposition with the sterile nature of the other rooms.

He closed the bathroom door and he saw the single shelf hidden behind it. And there was the gathering of prescription bottles and the torn packages of over-the-counter medications and he could not help but look. He recognized the names and the labels because they all had one thing in common. A mélange of pills to put you to sleep and keep you asleep and there were things he understood about her in that instant that no one else could realize and he wanted to walk out of the bathroom and go and knock on the bedroom door and tell her I am the same but he could not do that. If you exist in that haggard world you know better than to just ask someone why they don't sleep. Because there are two answers. There is the answer they want everyone to hear that makes sense. I always had trouble sleeping as a kid. I drink too much caffeine. I can't find the right pillow or the right mattress or my work schedule keeps me out of a good routine or the neighbors make too much noise or there is a streetlight outside my window that is too bright. There are all those reasons that pacify and explain to those who don't understand and then there are the real reasons that they don't want to talk about and are held inside and carried through the dark.

He looked at himself in the mirror. He wondered what kept her awake. He wondered how much longer he could go. How much longer before he collapsed into one of the undeniable sleeps he could not get out of and how much bad shit would happen without him knowing it and he stared deep into his own tired eyes and tried to find the bottom and as he felt himself begin to sink he fought to regain the determination to stay awake until there was some element of safety for the girl and for them and he wondered if that moment was even a possibility.

He finished his business and walked out of the bathroom and Cara was standing in the front room with her hands resting on the back of the sofa. Burdean came in from outside as Keal entered the room and they stood there and waited for her to say something. Her eyes were damp and she lowered her head and pursed her lips as if to push something down and then when she had gathered she looked at them.

"She doesn't know where she is. I had to tell her she's in Mississippi and that didn't mean anything to her. She doesn't know where her mother is and can't remember the last time she saw her. She doesn't know why people hide her or want her and she doesn't know exactly how long it has been going on."

Cara moved around the sofa and sat down.

"Men kill for her. And over her," Burdean said. "Men and women apparently."

"Nobody tells her anything," Cara said. "I asked her what she was doing in the cellar and she didn't know. She heard all the gunshots and hollering and screaming. She sat down in the corner and put her arms over her head and then it all went quiet. The door opened and Wanetah, that old woman, was standing there and she came in and stayed there with her until you two showed up."

"Is she made of gold?" Burdean said.

"I don't know what she's made of," Cara said. She wiped at her eyes.

Keal sat down beside her on the sofa. Burdean walked a circle.

"What's she doing now?"

"Sleeping. She's tired. She's scared."

"Join the club."

"She's a child."

Burdean took out his cigarettes. He tapped two out and he put one in his mouth and held up the other. Keal shook it off and Cara took it.

"We ain't supposed to smoke in the house," she said.

"We won't be after we finish these two," he said. He lit hers and his and then he sat down on the floor with his back slumped against the wall.

Cara rose from the sofa and she left the room and went into the kitchen.

"What you think?" Keal said. His voice low.

"I don't know. She could be lying."

"Lying about what?"

"About whatever, Keal. Who knows if the kid even said a word. She could be making it all up. I didn't hear nothing coming from in there."

"She came back in here upset. It's easy enough to see that."

"I reckon."

"I just don't get why she'd lie."

"Welcome to earth."

The faucet ran in the kitchen. Glasses clinked. Cara returned with the cigarette dangling from her mouth and carrying three glasses of water. She set them down on the floor by the sofa and took the cigarette from her mouth and then she said there was one other thing. I don't know if she's just wore out and talking out of her head or whatever but she said it right before she fell asleep.

"What was it?" Keal said.

"Something about the hand of God."

Burdean sat up straight. The two men looked at each other as if prodded.

"What about the hand of God?" Burdean said.

"I told you it was weird."

"No shit it's weird but what about it?"

Cara shook her head. Smoked. Burdean rose from the floor and Keal stood up from the sofa.

"She said she was part of it."

"Part of the hand," Burdean said.

"Yes."

"Of God."

"Yes."

"She told you that."

"Goddamn it. Yes. That's what they tell her. That's the only thing she could think of that they tell her."

"Who the fuck is they?"

"She don't know and I sure as hell don't know."

"A part of the hand of God. She said that."

"Yes yes yes. If I knew your name right now I'd scream at you."

Burdean walked into the other room and he took one of the table chairs and brought it back and sat down. Leaned over. His elbows resting on his knees. Cigarette between his fingers. A shadow of weariness creeping over him. For a moment he thought of being a younger man and working on one of those roofing crews in the hot ass sun and gasping for air through the humidity and sweating out whatever poison he had taken in the night before and then having to do it all again the next day and for the first time in his life he considered it with nostalgia.

"Speaking of names, did she tell you hers?" Keal asked.

"I didn't think to ask."

Cara picked up a glass of water and sat down again on the sofa. Keal stood with his arms folded and he walked over to the window, eyes into the night.

"Hey," Burdean said.

Keal turned around.

"Whatever road is in front of us, I get the feeling it's going to be rough. There isn't a right decision to be made. So I need you to go and lay down and get a few hours of sleep even if you don't want to. We don't need to be here when the sun rises and you have to be sharper than you are right now." Burdean spoke in a different voice. Almost kind. Eyeing the ribbon of smoke that trailed from the cigarette. Keal nodded.

"Go in there and lay that mattress on the floor," Cara said.

"Just a few hours," Keal said.

"Don't worry," Burdean said. "That's all we got."

"I'm going back in there with her," Cara said. She stood from the sofa and she stepped to Burdean and gave him her cigarette. Half of it still there. He took it and then she and Keal left Burdean alone. Cara's bedroom door opened and closed. The bumps of Keal sliding the mattress from behind the headboard and then dropping it on the floor in a whump. And then quiet.

Burdean stuck both cigarettes in his mouth and then he slid his chair over to the front door and opened it. He turned off the light so he could see outside better and he watched the night through the screen door. He then sat back down. A cigarette in each hand. His legs crossed. The hand of God is soaked in blood, he thought. And he wondered if it could be washed clean by this child.

27

Cara lay across two blankets folded on the floor next to the twin bed where the girl slept. The girl's breathing was heavy and cadenced. The only other piece of furniture in the room was a bedside table with a drawer and Cara had taken the lock of hair from her pocket and set it on the table before she lay down.

She stared at the ceiling. Her head propped on her arm behind her head. In one moment she considered the awful things the girl may have been exposed to and in the next she felt the power of providence that sent her driving down the right road at the right time and she was pacified that the girl was sleeping in the protection of the small bedroom instead of wherever she had been intended to sleep before they had discovered her.

The girl snorted in her sleep but she did not wake. Cara sat up on the floor. Stretched out her arm that had fallen asleep tucked under her head. She stretched and shook her arm and when the tingle was gone she reached over to the bedside table and picked up the lock of hair. She held it out in front of her in the draft of moonlight that filled the room.

She stood up from the floor. The blanket was down around the girl's waist on the twin bed and she lifted it and draped it across her shoulders. She then stood at the window and looked out into the night. She knew there was someone, somewhere, who loved the girl and wanted to know where she was and that this person was probably awake and staring into the same dark looking for some kind of answer.

She remembered the phone call to her grandmother, when she had been on her knees on the floor of the apartment in the moments after Madrid had reappeared and taken Lola away and her grandmother telling her to come and stay with me. Let me be with you and you be with me and the promise of that. And days later as she packed up and then started driving she imagined longdrawn summer evenings, sitting in lawn chairs with tall glasses of lemonade and sometimes a little gin. The smell of the kitchen. Being in the same house with someone who believed she was special.

She let the curl wrap around her crooked pinky finger. She had picked up the lock of hair from the salon floor as it had fallen from the snips of Lola's first haircut. One of those things you do in a moment without thinking and then it never leaves you. She had looked into the salon mirror at Lola and she had believed that she had stumbled upon something true. Something fundamental. Something so real that there was no way it wasn't going to find a way to hurt and as she stared out of the window and thought of the two men in the house and the lost girl asleep in her bed and the violent moment when she struck what could only have been a bad man with her car she marveled at how one thing could lead to another. There was always a miracle waiting to be performed.

28

Wayman was gifted with an unnatural patience, moving about the world with a casual fluidity as if he understood something about the workings of time that could not be explained in any other way than silent movement. The ragtag leather coat hid a lanky frame that mirrored his somnolent nature as if the skin and bones were bound together for the purpose of a lazy stroll and nothing else. He kept the watch in the front pocket of the leather coat and the dangling chain kept his hand entertained, twirling it while sitting at the bar or standing in line for a hamburger or pumping gas. When he pulled the watch out and opened it the time always read the same as it had not worked and he had not bothered to try and get it to work since the day he lifted it from the table at an estate sale while the grieving brother looked the other way.

He sat on a tree stump in the woods, a hundred yards away from Cara's house. He could see the squares of window light. He could hear the big car come along the road. He could hear the car doors thump shut through the country dark. He had seen the girl. He knew if they hadn't left in a rush then they had decided to believe they were safe. People did that when they were tired or when they were in over their heads and he figured they were both or else they wouldn't be at the house in the first place. They had done exactly what he thought they would do.

So he waited. He let them sink further into comfort and to pass the time he slid the tip of his index finger from pockmark to pockmark across his cheeks and around his neck, a skinlike trace of a map of everywhere he had been. Sometimes things seemed too easy and this was one of those times. He had missed the opportunity at the church to get the girl. Arriving too late. Finding the still and bloodied figures of those who were there for the same thing and then finding the cellar empty but before he left he had propped the bodies up next to one another on the church steps. Laughing a little as he left them there sitting politely as if they were a row of grim and obedient deacons waiting for the preacher to direct them to rise and gather the offering. But he sat in the dark now and reveled in the opportunity another twentyfour hours had provided. He was in no hurry and had seen enough in his life to know what destruction could arrive from running and rushing and hurrying and pushing and tripping over one another in haste. Only time was in possession of the answer.

Not far behind him the wolf sat on its haunches and watched Wayman with the same patience that Wayman watched the house.

The moonlight slashed through the trees and the night shadows fell across the earthfloor in sharp angles. Wayman was not aware of how long he had been sitting there and he was not concerned. There would be a moment that would speak to him. He was certain of that. And that moment arrived when the light went off in the front room of the house.

He pulled out the pocket watch and opened it. The hands stalled in time and space. There was nothing new that could happen and he didn't understand why more people could not come to this realization. The same things are born and the same things die and the same river flows and the same fire burns. The same hearts break and the same fools rise. There was a gift in such knowledge and he allowed it to carry him without regard to provocation or concern for consequence as if he was only a chess piece being moved about the world.

He clicked the watch shut and dropped it back into his pocket. Tucked the chain inside with it. He sat for a while longer. Surely they are not sleeping but surely they are, he thought. Little else on his mind. An owl hooted and a whippoorwill called and little things shuffled around in the dark and then he got up from the stump and joined the movement of the night as he began walking through the woods and toward the house and the wolf followed along.

29

Cara snuck out of the bedroom and left the girl sleeping. Burdean was not the watchdog he wanted to be and he sat slumped in the chair with his chin against his chest and he was out. She moved through the house with her hands on her hips and then she stopped in the doorway where Keal lay on the mattress. She pulled a band from her wrist and wrapped her hair on top of her head. She didn't believe he would be asleep but he was. She recognized the weariness in his eyes but she recognized other things as well. He was wearing his coat and wearing his boots and he was turned on his side with his hands folded underneath his cheek.

She took one step into the bare room where Keal slept. She maintained an argument with the depths of night, at one moment allowing it to warm her and make her believe that everything was as it should be and in other moments allowing it to push her into a great abyss where she fell wide-eyed and full of panic. She had begun to swallow the pills a year ago as a path to nighttime salvation but they had only sharpened the ups and downs.

She raised her hand and looked at her crooked fingers. Then she looked down at the floor and the shadow they made. She took one step closer to Keal and she began to whisper. In recent weeks she had found herself talking through the night. To who she didn't know. Angels, maybe. Maybe a little redhorned man with a pitchfork. She did not know and she did not care as she was pacified by hearing her own voice in the darkness and it carried her mind from the things that kept her awake and led her off into the realm of memories that did not hurt. She would not talk about Lola. She would talk about the day she sat on a tailgate on a lake shore, drinking cold cans of beer from a cooler and making fun of Anna Carruth turning halfdrunk cartwheels on a sandbar. She would talk about the afternoon she went to Jackson for reasons she couldn't remember and how she sat on the patio of some bar on an early spring day and the brownhaired and browneyed boy a few years younger who sat two tables away with his parents and while his mother and father tried to talk about whatever he was supposed to be doing in college he could not take his eyes off of her and she sat there after she was done eating and drank three glasses of tea waiting for him to get the nerve but he never did. She would talk about her grandmother and how as a child she would stand on a chair next to her in the kitchen, her grandmother making biscuits in a wooden bowl and letting Cara add the buttermilk and letting Cara stick her hands down into the bowl and mixing the pasty concoction and forming it into mighty clumps that became big and brown biscuits that they lathered in syrup and butter.

She spoke in her shadowfilled bedroom and described these memories with the precision of a journalist who only reported what had been seen without being privy to the emotions of the experience in the desire to protect herself from falling into a deeper melancholy. Sometimes it worked. Other times the recounting grabbed her with such sentiment that she would rise from the bed in frustration and go and walk up and down the road and listen to the chirps and calls of darkness to make herself forget again.

When she was alone she spoke in the normal volume of conversation but she whispered now to Keal, not wanting to wake him from the hardearned sleep. Not wanting Burdean to hear her. Suddenly filled with the desire for something secret. Maybe something special. But she did not relay a moment of contentment or wasted youth but told him another story, understanding why it wanted out. Accepting that there was something different about this night. About this speck of time. Her life felt like some torrent of what had been and what was to come and she wanted to let the things that mattered out of her even if no one was listening.

She crept further into the room. Whispering. There was this guy. I used to know him in high school. Fifteen or seventeen or however many years ago. I hadn't seen him since. But one night I came home and he was standing in my yard. Not doing anything but just standing there. It took me a second to recognize him. It would not have been so weird if it had been in the middle of the day, but it was the middle of the night. And this is a different town. It's a small world sometimes. I know that and I just figured he was now living around here and had seen me and was coming to say hello which was pretty much how he explained it when he started talking. I had been out at the bar for a while and the strangest thing is while I was driving home I had the feeling that somebody was going to be there. I didn't know who. Just felt like somebody was waiting on me and it scared me some. I turned around twice in the road and headed back toward town. But both times I told myself I was just imagining things and so both times I headed back home. And then there he was. I got out and he reminded me of his name and I didn't tell him to get the hell out of here like I should have. I kinda remembered him. I think we maybe went on a date or half a date or something one time. I had been living alone here for a while. Years, I think since my grandmother had died. So much quiet. So I was nice. Not nice in any crazy sort of way. Just hey how you doing and I gave him a hug and asked him if he wanted to come inside. Don't ever do that. I don't care who it is or when you saw them last or how good you know them. If they are standing in your yard at one in the morning don't let them inside the house.

She paused. Outside the tranquil night had begun to move, the limbs of the pecan tree being shoved by a sudden wind and the shadows swayed on the walls.

She held her damaged hand toward Keal and kept on. Still at a whisper. Because this is what happens when you let them in the house. He breaks your fingers and he does a lot of other things you don't want him to do before it's over with and then when they find him the back of his head is blown open because he put a shotgun in his mouth and so he doesn't even have to pay for it. Because you have to pay for it here. There is no heaven and hell. So he gets away with it and then you are left to stare at the ceiling and stare at the walls forfuckingever and wonder where it all came from. I don't know why I'm talking about this.

Even though you can't hear me. I've never talked about it. Not to nobody sleeping or nobody awake. Or maybe I do know why. Maybe it's because I had the feeling driving home that night that somebody was going to be here waiting for me. Maybe it lingers at the rim of every feeling I've had since Madrid returned and left with Lola. The anticipation of quick and unwelcome change. That is another story that I might tell you one day. I will tell you one day. But it is not the one that matters now. What matters now is that I knew what was going to happen with the man waiting in my yard and there was nothing I could do to stop it. I saw it coming from a mile away. From ten miles away. Not the specifics but the calamity. I've always wondered at that, how something could travel across time without any inclination or reason and just happen as if it had always been programmed into the spinning of the earth and all you can do is take it. I didn't decide it. It was coming and I felt it and it was as real as the sun and I swore if I ever had that feeling again that I would do everything I could to stop it. To change whatever was happening. I have that feeling right now and I've had it since the second I woke up last night and believed something was wrong with Wanetah. I believed something was wrong in the night and there is still something wrong in the night and it has gathered itself in the flesh and blood of that girl. Something beyond anything we can understand. That's what I believe. And I will do whatever I can to help her because there is nothing else.

She then reached up and pulled the band from her hair and it fell across her shoulders. As if it had been necessary to get it out of the way to say what she needed to say. Keal turned from his side and lay on his back and his hand began to twitch in his sleep. Then his head began to flop from side to side. Outside the wind gained strength and roared across the land and she could not know that Keal was dreaming the same dream from before. The clouds and then the rain and then the silence and the lightning smacking the sky and he was running toward the building. And while Cara was emptying herself into the dark and while Keal was tousling through the dream and while Burdean slept sitting in the chair and while the wind rushed through the trees, none of them heard the latch pried open on the Volkswagen and none of them saw or heard the man in the long leather coat reach into the trunk and pull out a five-gallon tank of gasoline. None of them saw or heard as he walked a circle around the house, muted by the wind. Singing a little song to himself. Pouring the gasoline on the ground and making a ring around the house and then tossing the can and standing there in the gathering wind with the coat flapping and his slick hair being pushed around his head and grinning at the absurdity of the world.

Keal woke with a jerk and a yelp when the lightning of his dreams struck the building and set it ablaze and it startled Cara and she stepped back. Slipped out of the room before he noticed her there. Burdean came alive at the same time, waking and slapping his own face in aggravation with having fallen asleep. When Cara opened the bedroom door to check on the girl she was no longer in the bed but she was standing at the window with her arms raised and she was watching the limbs of the pecan tree bend in the wind and none of them realized the man in the coat was standing outside the house but when he lit the pack of matches and dropped it on the ground they all heard the flush and they all saw the earth rise in flame.

30

The wind fueled the fire encircling the house and the flames spread across the dry grass and dead leaves of autumn and then it ran into the azaleas and ignited the bushes. A flaming possum streaked across the yard and Wayman watched with amusement as it ran headfirst into the mailbox post and then writhed and twisted and then finally steadied into a hot little lump in the middle of the road.

The lights came on inside and Wayman saw them running around in a panic trying to figure out what to do. He watched them with his head cocked to the side as if studying a painting. Cara had the girl by the hand and Keal and Burdean were running from window to window, looking out and trying to see who had done this and where to break and then Burdean laid eyes on Wayman. Standing there illuminated by the flames with his head cocked and a demented and firestroked expression. The wind howled and Burdean shouted to the others and then Cara and the girl darted for the kitchen. Burdean shouted something else to Keal and then Burdean came out of the front door firing wild into the dark and Wayman moved only to leisurely reach inside his coat and pull a gun from a holster in the cocksure certainty that no bullet would find him and then he aimed unhurried as if trying to win a carnival prize and he fired.

Burdean was hit and he stumbled across the ring of fire and just when Wayman was about to shoot again Burdean collapsed face first onto the ground. Keal shouted from behind the window and Wayman laughed a little and shot out the glass as Keal ducked and then he shot out the rest of the windows, shattering explosions that put Cara and the girl down on the kitchen floor and Cara was crawling into the front room to see if Keal was alive or dead when he raised his head and yelled for her to stay with the girl. She turned and scurried back but she only found the kitchen door open and the girl was gone.

Wayman saw her small figure appear from behind the house, leaping without hesitation through the flames and running for the woods. He watched her for a moment. Admired her. He knew nobody else had a gun or they would be shooting it so he returned his pistol to the holster and he began to walk away from the chaos he had created, looking back over his shoulder with the tinge of regret that he could not stay and admire it longer. He took one more look at the smoldering possum and then he shifted his attention to the girl and he began running after her with his long and lanky strides and he was closing in on her hustling little body when he heard Cara coming behind them, calling out. Wayman stopped and pulled the pistol and fired at her silhouette and she hit the ground and lay flat in the darkness. He then saw the younger man dragging the older man away from the spreading fire and Wayman fired at the younger in a quick succession of shots that sent him running back into the house. It was then that Wayman turned back to the girl and he knew she had disappeared into the shadows of the treeline.

He entered the woods, slipping through the spaces between the hardwoods and hackberries and pines. Leaves falling and limbs bending and the entirety of the darkwood seemed to sway along with the strength of the wind in some impromptu but orchestrated performance. He watched for her small figure. Stopping and listening. Watching some more. And then he saw her move from behind one tree and to another. He stepped in her direction and paused. Waiting for her to do it again and she did. Her small dark figure shifting from tree to tree and he stood with his arms crossed and watched her, entertained by her belief that she was getting away. He looked back to see if anyone was coming but if they were he couldn't find them through the trees and he knew it was time to get the girl and be done with this. He crept toward her. Thinking to call to her and tell her she was going to be okay. I'm not going to hurt you. But not wanting to send her running before he knew he could catch her and then she did just that as she darted from behind the tree and ran harder and ran deeper and he chased after her. Lowlimbs slapping his head and her short steps making quick navigation and he was not as agile as he barreled through the limbs and brush but his size mattered. They came to a shallow creek and she went down the slope and splashed across the muddy bottom and she was coming up the other side when she slipped and went down to her knees and this gave him the moment he needed to catch her. She crawled up the bank and was rising to her feet again when he dove and grabbed her by the ankle and she kicked and fought but he held on tight. Got both hands on her and then straddled her with his knees and he held her pinned to the ground and said quit kicking. Ain't nobody gonna hurt you if you'll stop all this nonsense. Just listen to me. She kept squirming and kicking but she was caught and trapped and then as if struck by some instant resolution, the fight left her and she lay there motionless.

He brushed his slick hair back from his face. Leaned in close to her and said you're going with me little lady. I'm gonna get up and then you're gonna get up real nice and easy. Behaving exactly like you're behaving right now without no fight or any other ridiculousness and if you do that then we won't have not one problem in this whole world. But he never had a chance to get up. The wolf came in a silent streak, its jaws clamping around the back of his neck and tackling him off the girl. When Wayman's weight tumbled from her she rose and ran again and left them in a growling and screaming and tangled mess of man and animal. Fangs and claws as they rolled together and Wayman punched and pried and wrestled the wolf from his neck and shoved it away. He felt the blood run warm down his shoulders and chest and the wolf snarled, its bluewhite eyes and teeth reflecting the moonlight and before he could get to his gun the hunter pounced again and somewhere in the struggle for life Wayman managed to find his knife inside his pants pocket and he fought the wolf with one hand and opened the blade with the other and the great wail of the wolf blended with the howl of the wind as the sharp steel sunk into the soft fur and flesh of its breast.

31

Cara ran back to the house and quickly doused the burning azaleas with a garden hose and Keal dragged Burdean inside. He was shot through the left shoulder and bleeding fast and when Cara tempered the fire she came back inside and ripped a towel and tried to tie him up and slow the flow. Burdean grimaced and grunted and spit and ripped out a string of cuss words in a long and breathless growl.

"Goshdamn man. I thought you were dead," Keal said.

"I figured I should play that way if I didn't want to get shot again."

Cara pulled the tourniquet tighter and Burdean let it rip again and when he was done he told Keal to quit pissing around and go after the child. I ain't getting shot for nothing. Keal grabbed Burdean's pistol and took off into the woods.

Everything looked the same in every direction. The woods an infinity. He tried to calm and tried to think as he traipsed aimlessly and then he stopped and he worked to marry this moment to what he had seen now twice in the lightningstruck dream. There is a message or a direction in it but what is it and all he could muster in the windswept night was a greater desperation. He wandered through a new strangeness, a suspension without form or time and he felt the living and the dead, the real and the imagined, the dreamed and the lived. There was nothing to trust but the world itself so he kept going and kept believing he would be guided to the girl by whatever had guided him this far and then he heard the wolf scream.

He moved in what he thought was the direction of the cry and then he was led closer by the long howl of agony. A mournful hymn of reckoning for what is to come. He came to the creek and he saw the wolf in the moonlight, lying on its side and offering a last song to its hill country home. He crossed the creek splashing through the same steps as the girl and Wayman. He climbed the bank and approached with caution but the wolf was done. It lay panting, trying to howl now but only mustering a whimper. Blood down its chest and covering its coat and front legs.

Keal knelt and watched it die.

He was rising from his knee when he saw the silver pocket watch in the moonlight glint. He picked it up from the leaves and it was wet with blood and he wiped his hand on the ground and then wiped the watch on the ground. He clicked it open and clicked it closed and clicked it open and closed. Stuck it in his pocket and he began walking again. There was no wolf to guide him and no old woman and no footprints to follow in the layers of leaves and no way to see the trail of blood that dripped from the tips of Wayman's fingers as he slouched through the woods and there was no sound but the rush of the wind but he started anyway and now he was calling out, thinking if she heard him then she would call back and who gives a shit if the guy in the coat hears me because this is all on the edge of the end anyway and it's been on the edge of the end since it all started and he moved through the woods with more haste and less caution and he called out. Hey. Hey. Where are you? Where are you? Just holler back. Hey. He moved and called out and his path was wandering and futile and after half an hour he finally quit calling. He sat down on the trunk of a fallen pine. The night seemed to grow colder as he sat. His breath appeared before him and he tucked his hands in his coat pockets, relinquishing his grip on the pistol. Somewhere in the remoteness he thought he heard the howl of the wolf but he knew that could not be. He could think of nothing other than this is over and done with.

He was buried in his worry for the girl and the failure of it all when he began to think of his mother and the mold and he did not notice when the wind stopped. It came in an instant and a hush fell over the dark country as if a spell of silence had been cast. He only noticed it when the hush was broken with a nightbird's song, the solitary call of life continuing on. He lifted his head that had dropped in exasperation and looked around. The night had changed in a moment and he was struck by the clarity of his recent dream. The rain that fell soft and gentle and then stopped and how quickly the world grew solemn and then how quickly the world turned turbulent when the storm rose and the lightning cracked. The intensity of change. And like he had done so many times in his life he felt the connection between what he saw and felt when he dreamed and what he saw and felt in the waking hours and he stood from the trunk of the fallen pine with the pulse of hope that whatever this thing was that they had gotten into was not dead but alive and the message had come in the shift and sudden tilt of nature. And if he could have seen with the eyes of God he would have seen the girl beneath a short ridge not far from where he was standing. Hidden by the leafless and grayed kudzu vines that draped over the edge of the ridge like a gnarled shroud, sitting with her knees pulled to her chest and her head leaned back against the red clay earthwall and when she had started to calm herself after she was safe from the chase of the slickhaired man, the wind had calmed with her.

32

Cara hurriedly helped Burdean get situated. The bullet had gone through his shoulder and the bleeding had been slowed by the tourniquet. He was leaned back on the sofa, hurt and grumbling and sweating and smoking. She had crafted a makeshift sling with scissors and a bath towel and replaced his bloodied shirt with an oversized sleep shirt. She told him to keep his arm still if he wanted the bleeding to quit though she had no idea if that was true or not. Outside the fire had diminished into a smolder and become a red ring of burnt ground, flakes of ash and ember rising and twirling away and the smoke settled around the house and seeped into the woods. Cara took a flashlight and a hammer from a kitchen drawer and she told Burdean if he didn't think he was going to die then she was going to help find the girl.

"I ain't going to die," he said. "I guess the plan is to smack him with a hammer."

"If he gets close enough."

When she was gone he repeated the line to himself. I ain't going to die. I ain't going to die. But he wasn't sure he believed it. Not from being shot in the shoulder but from all this other crazy ass shit that was going on around him. He stood up from the sofa and went into the kitchen. He tried to be a good patient and he kept his left arm stationary in the sling and with his right hand he found a glass in the cabinet and then he rifled through every other cabinet looking for something to drink besides wine. There was nothing else and so he dropped his cigarette in the sink and he picked up the bottle of red from the counter. He pulled the cork out with his teeth and he ignored the glass and drank from the bottle, a little trail of burgundy down the side of his mouth and disappearing into his beard.

He walked back into the front room. He slid the chair over to the sofa and he sat down on the sofa and propped his feet up in the chair. In some other time he would have been a vision of tranquility with the wine bottle propped on his thigh and the extended pose of relaxation. But he was damaged and felt as if he was being pulled down into some great depth where there was no bottom to be found.

I don't know what else you expected, he thought. He did not lack selfawareness. For the most part he knew what he was and he was not completely surprised that even considering the current extremity, his life had led him to sitting on this sofa in this night with this gunshot wound through his shoulder. You have been doing things in the night for a long time. You have laid knuckles to noses. You have gone in doors and taken things. You have cornered and intimidated scared men who pissed off the wrong people and you enjoyed it. You have made a shoddy living doing shoddy things. It made sense.

He tried to think back to something he had been good at. Or someone he had been good for. Or when he had been anything more than a grunt or a gunsel and all he could muster was his memories of baseball. He wasn't skilled at the game as a whole but he could always hit. He couldn't field a position with any fluidity and his arm was mediocre on its best day but he could always hit. Something about the grip on the bat and the ball coming out of the pitcher's hand and being able to recognize the spin of the seams and the break of the ball and the timing of contact and the quick snap of his wrists that brought the barrel around in a split second stroke of violence that drove the ball and the great satisfaction of hard contact that made him feel like he knew something that nobody else knew. The only secret he believed he had ever known. And every year that the winter died and the seasons shifted into spring he felt the urge to grab a bat as if he was a boy again, staring out of the window at school, counting the hours until the bell rang and it was time to go out to the ballfield. Every few years he wandered into the batting cage at the county fair and dropped coins into the pitching machine to see if he could still do it and he could still do it even at the age when most things had slowed down.

He felt that pulse and he felt that secret knowledge and the last time he had been to the batting cage he had tried to share it. Waiting his turn while a high school kid wearing a high school practice jersey took big and empty swings but every third or fourth pitch he actually made contact and then he'd say something full of bravado to his two buddies who stood on the outside of the cage. Burdean leaned on his bat and watched, a little more irritated with each swing and miss and then he couldn't take it anymore.

"Hey," he said to the kid.

The kid looked over to him.

"Keep your front shoulder closed."

"What?"

"Keep your front shoulder closed. It's opening up and you can't hit it hard when you're all opened up."

"That right?" the kid said.

"That's right."

"What do you know?"

"I know how to hit a baseball which is more than I can say for you."

"They had baseball back in your day?"

"Back in my day. Funny."

Another pitch came. Another swing and a feeble pop up.

"I'm telling you," Burdean said. He walked over to the cage door where the friends stood. The pitches kept coming and the kid never changed his swing and Burdean kept offering bits of unwelcome advice. When the meter ran out, the kid turned and looked at Burdean and said maybe you could just shut the fuck up. He opened the cage door and stepped out and he threw the bat on the ground in irritation and then he turned to his buddies and said I can't wait until I'm old and I get to tell people who ain't interested in my opinion how to do shit. The buddies laughed and Burdean felt a surge.

"You pigheaded little shit," Burdean said.

"Go ahead. Tell me some more, Babe Ruth. Tell me some more shit you can do that's so great."

More laughter.

Burdean lifted his bat and laid it on his shoulder and he took a serious step toward the three of them. Situated on the threshold of rage. They were brave in the moment. Young and brave. And he was going to find out if they could hold it. He then raised the bat from his shoulder and pointed it at them and said I can tell you three more things I can do better than any of you can currently do or will ever be able to do. Drink and fight and fuck.

None of them spoke. Burdean waited for any excuse to turn into a storm. A word or an eyeroll or a snippet of laughter but the kid didn't offer. The smartest of the three grabbed the other two by the arms and they all backed away and slunk off across the fairgrounds.

He turned up the bottle now and drank and then he laughed remembering the looks on their boyish faces. The laughter made his shoulder hurt a little more and so he chugged again. Drink and fight and fuck. He realized that's all he had ever really wanted to do and what a nice and simple life it had been. But he could feel the fight going out of him.

He wondered what was going on in the woods. He knew this could be over already. The girl stolen away by whoever that man was and tomorrow would return to the simplicity of the things he craved. And he also knew that bullet could have just as easily landed right between his eyes and if by some miracle they returned to the house with the girl then there was a decision to be made.

He kicked the chair away and he got up from the sofa. He swigged from the bottle once more and then he set it on the floor and he lit a cigarette. He had watched his father get up at the same time every morning and pack the same ham sandwich and cheese and crackers and thermos of coffee into his lunch pail and then drive off down the same road and spend ten hours walking the same steps at the same sawmill every single day and he knew his father had done this because he had no choice and because he cared about his son and his wife but it taught Burdean he'd better have a choice and he might be better off if he didn't care. He felt that now. He had done it. He had escaped that life with apathy in one hand and risk in the other and he thought about his father and how quickly he had grown old and it made him detest the normal expectations of men and women even more than he already did. He paced around the room. Smoking and thinking and it occurred to him there were many more beers to drink and many more cigarettes to smoke and many more women in many more hazy bars and that seemed worth staying alive for. But there would be a cost. There was always a cost even in the dog's life he had been living.

He walked into the kitchen. He stared at the phone on the wall. A few numbers dialed and a few words spoken and this could be over and done with. He shifted his eyes to the crucifix hanging next to the phone and then he reached for the receiver but his hand moved instead to the crack in the crucifix and he ran his finger along the break. And he thought the imperfection made more sense to him than any perfect cross or marble angel or handsome Jesus he had ever seen. The flaw in it. The brokenness. The revelation that there is nothing pure and the relief that comes when you understand you cannot attain the impossible. And he was far beyond trying to attain the impossible.

He moved his finger from the broken crucifix and he lifted the receiver and dialed. It answered after the first ring and before there was a word uttered on the other end Burdean said all I want you to do is listen and listen good. Tell me how much will you pay for her. And I will hang up and find another buyer if you tell me we already have a deal because that deal was off the second I figured out that the package I was supposed to pick up in the cellar was a child standing in the middle of this goddamn nightmare.

33

Keal saw the dot of light moving through the trees and he waited while it moved closer in his direction. The flashlight beam waved through the dark and was carried in silence but when it was twenty yards away he could see that it was Cara and he called out. It's me don't shoot.

"I don't have a gun, you dummy," she called back.

"I wouldn't say that so loud."

"If he was in earshot we'd know it."

"What do you have?"

"A hammer and don't say nothing about it."

She put the light on his face as if to make sure it was him and he held up his hand to shield his eyes. She moved closer and lowered the flashlight.

"Where is she?" she asked.

"I don't know."

"What the hell."

"I'm trying. Look. I found this back there by a dead wolf."

"A dead wolf?"

He held the pocket watch in the palm of his hand. She shined the light on it, the watch smeared in dirt and blood.

"Whose blood?" she said.

"I think the wolf. It looks like it was stabbed a couple of times."

"Shit."

"Yeah. Shit," he said.

"You didn't see nothing or hear nothing?"

"I heard the wolf holler when it happened."

"Why the hell would he stop to kill a wolf?"

"You can add that to the list of things I don't know."

She raised the flashlight and scanned the woods.

"I've been calling but she won't answer," he said.

"They didn't just disappear."

"It sure as hell looks like it. Where's Burdean?"

"Sitting at the house trying not to bleed."

They began again together. Calling out and searching without any notion what direction to go in and feeling the helplessness of it all. Cara stopped once and said I can't hardly think about what is going to happen to her. I should have never left her alone in the kitchen, not even for a second.

Keal felt for her in that moment.

"Don't do that," he said.

"I can't help it."

"There ain't no rhyme or reason to any of this. And if she hadn't run we'd probably all be dead."

The girl had seen the dot of light through the tangle of kudzu vines just as Keal had seen it and she had slipped out from her hiding place beneath the ridge and started following them. Listening to them call. Stopping when they stopped. Hearing their voices but not getting close enough to make clear what they were saying. Once Cara had turned in a circle with the flashlight and the girl tucked herself behind a tree as the beam spun in her direction. A black comedy version of hide-and-seek.

They lapped back around and ended up at the creek. Neither had spoken for a long time. Neither called out for the girl anymore. Keal asked for the flashlight and they followed the creekbank until they came to the wolf. The dark began to weaken, the faintest of light dusting the eastern sky. The early birds awakened, fluttering about and chirping their sweet songs of starting over. One by one the stars began to slip away into another night.

Keal and Cara paused over the wolf. The blood had stopped running from its wounds and had turned from red to the deepest of crimson and matted its fur. He turned off the flashlight and set it and the pistol on the ground. He then reached over and stroked the wolf's backside in a gesture of passing and he wondered if the wolf's spirit would stay in this land where it hunted and stalked and slept and howled at the moon or if there was some wolfish otherworld with fresh scents and smells and easy prey. Cara made several steps away and then she lay down on her back, staring up through the colorless and leafless limbs and into the farreaching blue of forever. He searched for something to say to her and she searched for something to say to him but they only shared the despondence without the weakness of words.

They heard the footsteps coming toward them at the same

time. Keal reached for the pistol and Cara sat up quickly and they both rose to their knees. He was holding the pistol pointed at the vague figure approaching them when Cara reached over and touched his hand and lowered it. The girl came closer and her small figure gained clarity and she stopped in front of them. Keal picked up the flashlight and illuminated her face, the corners of her mouth upturned in a tightlipped grin.

34

The motel was a squat row of eight rooms and sat at the end of a diminishing stretch of liquor stores and smoke shops and a boarded up juke joint. The last stop or the first stop of the town limits depending on which way you were going. The dark highway stretched out into the night and the great big mouth of blackness reached to swallow the last room of the row. A light shined from the motel office and a chain-smoking woman with curlers in her hair sat in a swivel chair that creaked with the habitual movement of hand to mouth. She wore a fuzzy robe and fuzzy slippers and she was watching a scary movie she had seen a handful of times so there was nothing scary about it. She knew when the bad man in the mask would appear from the dark and she knew who was going to get it and she knew when to look away when the gore was more than she could handle.

Only two of the eight rooms were occupied and all eight

rooms were the same. Two beds and shaggy green carpet and plastic curtains. She always booked the rooms starting from the far end so she could better ignore the shouts and sights of the comings and goings and she sat content in her smoke and solitude as the night had been quiet and looked like it was going to stay that way. She dabbed out the cigarette in an ashtray on the desk and picked a flake of crust from the chicken bone left in the greasy box and it had hit the time of night when she could doze if she wanted and she felt it coming on. She turned down the volume on the television and she tapped the screen. He's right there, she thought. Trying to tell the young woman that the thing of nightmares was waiting for her on the other side of the closet door.

She spun around in the chair and looked out of the office window as the headlights appeared from the highway. Little bright eyes rising out of the dark. She got up and turned off the overhead light in the office in hopes that the car would keep going and she felt the irritation when it slowed and turned into the parking lot. But there would be no more work to do as she recognized the car as belonging to one of the two occupants. It parked at the end of the row. The headlights turned off and she waited for someone to climb out but the silhouette behind the wheel only sat there for what felt like a long time though all stillness felt like a long time in the pit of the night. She folded her arms and wondered. The driver was alone or she would have otherwise figured there were dirty things going on inside the car that couldn't wait for the closed door of the room. Dirty or illegal or both. She gave it another minute and when nothing happened she sat back down in the swivel chair. The man in the mask had killed the young woman and was moving along the treelined sidewalk in a slow stalk with blood dripping from the blade as the one-note hum promised there would be more carnage to come.

With the volume turned low she heard the bump of the car door closing. She looked back out of the window and she saw him in the meager light of the parking lot. The claw rips down the sleeves of the leather jacket and the bloodsoaked shirt and the hair falling around the bloodied face of the hanging head. He limped to the front of the car and stopped. Leaned against it as if he had taken a last step. Then he peeled off the jacket and dragged it along the ground as he limped on to the door of the motel room. There was blood down his arms and down his back and she rose from the chair and put her face close to the window as if to make sure she was seeing what she saw. He made it to the door and he dropped the jacket. He pulled the room key from his pocket and unlocked the door and he collapsed inside. His feet sticking out of the open door.

She had seen enough happen in this parking lot and in these rooms to know better than to get close so she picked up the phone and dialed the room number. It rang and rang as she watched the feet in the doorway. They did not move and then she hung up. There was a first aid kit in the bottom drawer of the desk and she lifted it out and then she picked up the phone to call an ambulance but before she dialed she saw the feet move and slip inside the room. And then a bloodied arm reached out and dragged the jacket inside and the door closed. She lit another cigarette and paced around the office and then she grabbed the first aid kit. She left the office and walked down the breezeway, shuffling through the shadows in her slippers and not wanting to be a part of any of this and overcome with the feeling that she was next in line for the man in the mask but she fought back her dread and she set the first aid kit by the door.

She knocked. The room was dark but then a lamp turned on and gave a pallid glow around the edge of the closed curtains. She knocked again and then hurried away and when she got back inside the office the man in the mask was killing again and she clicked off the television. She stood there in the grayblack and watched the room and just as she was reaching for the phone again the motel room door opened and the same bloodied arm reached out and pulled the first aid kit inside.

35

Burdean hung up the phone. He leaned on the kitchen counter. Rubbed at his beard. He held the cigarette between his fingers with his eyes lost in distant thought. The voice had been like he remembered. Deadpan. Cold. A voice that used very few words to get its point across. He wanted to ask if this was the man with the sideburns but with each word the man spoke, Burdean felt a sinking feeling. The feeling of being lowered into a well. And before he hit bottom he had to get off the phone. That and he knew the motherfucker would lie anyway.

The money that had been offered for the girl was more than Burdean had imagined it would be. By a lot. Between the offer and the two rolls of cash he had kept from the old woman it was enough money for him to leave this place and quit doing these shit jobs for these shit people for a damn long time. He had no idea what made this little girl so important and so valuable and so dangerous but she was all of those things and when he had asked for that detail on the phone the voice said you have your new deal like you wanted and then the phone hung up.

Part of him wanted them to return with the girl but another part of him wanted her to be gone so he didn't have to decide what he was going to do. Though he knew he had made his decision when he picked up the telephone and made the call. Pilate with his hands wringing.

He returned to the front room and he picked up the wine bottle and he walked outside. The charred earth. The blackened bushes. The cloud of smoke that held the house and eased across the land and the changing light of a morning to come. It all gave him the sensation that he had crossed a border into some strange country where there were no laws and no language that he could understand and he stared out toward the road and he imagined an old man struggling along, a hunched back and the gait of the lonely and he did not need to see the old man's face to know he was imagining himself. Not far from now. Nothing seemed far from now anymore as there was nothing but the implausible surrounding him. Age and death appeared through the smoke in the unwelcome reflection of life to come. The time when his lusts could no longer be filled and there had been nothing done between those lusts worth remembering. He raised the wine bottle and finished it off and then with his mediocre arm he threw the bottle toward the apparition and the bottle busted in the road and the image disappeared. He grabbed at his shoulder, throbbing now with the twist of the throwing motion and then he slipped off the sling and tossed it on the ground where a scattering of leaves still burned. The cloth of the makeshift sling caught fire and he watched it burn and he did not believe that Keal and the woman had the girl or they would have returned.

He felt inside his shirt and touched the bloodsoaked tourniquet and he couldn't find any reason not to get in the big car and
drive away. They had the Volkswagen and they could make their
own decisions and he thought he needed to apologize to Keal
and if he ever saw him again he promised himself that he would.
Maybe one day they would be in the same bar or at the same
gas station and he would tell Keal I got us both into more than
I thought we were getting into and Keal would slap him on the
shoulder and maybe they would laugh or maybe they would just
look at each other with the satisfaction of having survived. The
only thing he wanted right now was his pistol back but it would
not be difficult getting another one and he was a little drunk
and very tired and wholly resigned and relieved that all of this
was coming to the end without having to betray anyone and he
started across the yard and to the big car.

The three figures emerged from the woods and through the
smoke like spirits rising. He had his hand on the handle of the
car door when he saw them. A small figure between two larger
figures. He mumbled to himself in disbelief. And then he had a
brief conversation in which he acknowledged the inevitability
of their appearance. A band of gold appeared across the horizon
and stretched into the blue and the sky held the easy light as if to
offer the dawn as a respite. Burdean watched them walk through
the smoke and across the charred ground and when Cara draped
her arm around the girl's shoulder, he felt an unfamiliar sensation as a great sense of pity washed over him. For what had been
done. And for what was to come.

MORNING

36

Cara walked inside the house and set the hammer on the windowsill in the front room. The girl reached inside the big car and took out the framed angel and she waved at Cara to come back outside. She then took Cara's hand and pulled her away from the men and they moved across the yard in the ashen light. There was smoke and there was the morning mist and there was the haze of earliest day. The vagaries of the natural world lending itself to their slipping hold on reality. The girl told her about the wolf attacking the man, that the last thing she saw was them tangled together in an ugly fight and then she got away and kept running until she hid behind the vines. Burdean and Keal sat on the hood of the big car with their feet resting on the fender and watched them. Every now and then the girl would look over to the men as if to make sure they were still there.

"Why won't she talk to me or you?" Burdean said.

"I don't know. It's a wonder she talks at all. I've only seen the last two days of her life but it'd be enough to shut me up."

"If that's what it takes then I wish there was somebody hunting and hiding you."

"Nice," Keal said. "Shoulder hurt?"

"Yep."

"You need a doctor?"

"Nope."

Keal pushed his hair back away from his face. Rubbed his bloodshot eyes.

"You think she's ever been to school?"

"Don't know."

"I bet she hasn't. But she looks smart in a I-know-something-you-don't kind of way."

Burdean looked at him and Keal recognized the expression. Burdean wanted him to stop talking but he wasn't ready.

"You see how she carries that angel drawing around?"

"I can't say I've noticed. I been paying more attention to who might be coming through the door or up the road or around the corner trying to kill us."

"She does. She held it up and pointed at it when we first got out here and you went inside to check it all out."

"So."

"Maybe she's something like that."

"Like an angel," Burdean said.

"That'd be one good reason people want her."

"And there's about a million other reasons that make a lot more goddamn sense."

"You said she must be important," Keal said.

"That don't appear to be at question but I didn't say she had wings."

"Angels on earth don't have wings."

"Please. I'm begging you. If there is one and only one thing you will do for me the rest of your life please don't start telling me everything you think you know about angels."

"I just wonder why she seems drawn to it."

Burdean shrugged. Lit a cigarette.

"I get the notion she don't have nothing and maybe never has," he said. "Maybe it's just something to hold on to. You probably had something you dragged around as a kid."

"Maybe," Keal said.

"You should have never took the frame in the first place."

"Too late for that."

"I've told you never to take nothing from a job we're doing."

"We took the money rolls."

"That's different."

"That's what I thought you'd say."

Cara and the girl paused in their conversation. They looked over at the men and then the girl took Cara's arm and moved them several more steps away. Then the girl raised her hand and made a slow circular motion toward the sky.

"I hate to keep asking this but what are we going to do?" Keal said.

"Ed has this fishing camp, not too far from the truckstop. Just a couple of rooms on stilts but I think we go there and stay for a few days. Won't nobody know we're there."

"Nobody but Ed."

"He won't say nothing."

"All he does is talk, according to you."

"Ed flaps his gums pretty much without cease but he has never said a word about any job he did with me. He knows the difference between talking and talking about the wrong thing."

Cara walked with the girl to the front door and the girl went inside, carrying the framed drawing. Cara came over to the car and they both hopped off the hood. Cara had found gauze in the bathroom and she instructed Burdean to take off his coat and shirt. She made him a better bandage and then she tied a fresh tourniquet around his wound. He grimaced through it all and then he put the coat and shirt back on.

"I'm gonna make her something to eat. You two want something?"

"How about you start with the important stuff instead," Burdean said.

"Okay. Whoever that was chasing her caught up with her. Then a wolf jumped on him and she got away."

Burdean looked up into the sky. Shook his head.

"A wolf jumped on him and she got away," he said.

"That's right."

"That would explain it," Keal said.

"Are you serious?" Burdean said.

Cara and Keal nodded.

"I can't believe I'm about to ask this but did the wolf kill him?"

"She didn't say," Cara said. "But me and him saw the wolf and there wasn't anybody laying there beside it."

Keal pulled the pocket watch from his coat. He showed it to Burdean and said this was on the ground next to the wolf.

He opened the latch and the three of them looked at the hands mired in time.

"You think that time is meant to be a.m. or p.m.?" Keal said.

"Does it have anything on it like initials?" Burdean said.

"No."

"I'd say p.m.," Cara said.

"It don't really fucking matter now does it," Burdean said and he snatched the watch away from Keal. He closed it and tossed it in the open window of the big car.

"Settle down," she said.

"Settle down."

"Yeah."

"Settle down. That's really what you want to say."

"Yeah."

"Well you ain't the one shot. Are you?"

"Look at my damn house. Look at my damn yard."

Burdean tapped out a cigarette. He pursed his lips and kept shaking his head but then he let it fall though he wanted to let it rip.

"All right. Fine," he said. "We all got problems."

"Tell her about the fishing camp," Keal said.

Burdean told her.

"I'm not leaving here," Cara said.

"You don't have to. But she is," Burdean said. He pointed toward the house where the girl was standing in one of the shot-out windows, watching them.

"Why don't you want to leave?" Keal said.

"I just don't. Let her stay here with me."

"Do you think this shit is over?" Burdean said. "This shit

is at the beginning and if you believe anything other than that then you're nuts. You can stay out of it if you want but we're going to the camp and the kid is going with us. If anybody wants to quit then quit. Same goes for you, Keal."

"What did I say?"

"You didn't say nothing. Just know it. We ain't a family and don't nobody here owe nobody nothing."

Cara dismissed Burdean with a wave of her hand and she turned and went inside the house. Through the broken window they watched her kneel down and talk to the girl. Cara had softened as she spoke to her, a comforting and consoling demeanor. The girl then nodded to Cara and then the both of them came back out of the house, holding hands. They stopped in front of Burdean and Keal.

"Do you want to tell them or do you want me to?" Cara asked her. The girl looked up at her with hesitant eyes. She shrugged. And then Cara encouraged her. You can do it. It's okay. You can tell them. But the girl cupped her hand and leaned to Cara's ear and she whispered.

"Okay," Cara said. "I'll tell them."

"Tell us what?" Burdean said.

"We're going to tell you what is so important about her. At least as far as what she's been told. It's probably best if everybody knows everything."

"I thought we already asked for all this particular information," Burdean said.

"You did."

"Then why are we just now getting it?"

"She didn't feel like telling it then."

"So when did she tell it to you?"

"Right over there in the yard. Just now."

Burdean looked at Keal.

"Keal thinks she fell out of heaven."

"I didn't say that. Not exactly. I swear."

"Stop swearing."

"Do you two want to hear this or not?" Cara said.

"God yes. Let's have it."

Cara took a deep breath and gave the girl a glance of reassurance.

"Well?" Keal said.

"They believe she can control the weather," Cara said.

Burdean took a long drag on the cigarette. It was far more ridiculous than what Keal was thinking but then he remembered the amount of money he had been offered to deliver the girl and he couldn't do anything but laugh. He started laughing and then he laughed harder and they all stood there and waited until he had laughed himself into a surge of pain in his wound. He then grimaced and grabbed at his shoulder before he finally gathered his breath.

"Does she also fly and turn water into wine?" he said.

Keal had not laughed. While Burdean had allowed the absurd to grab hold, Keal had kept his eyes on the darkhaired child. The revelation and the reaction had no effect on her as she stood with the expression of the unsurprised. Keal was filled with wonder at the mere suggestion that such a thing could even be possible. He leaned down to the girl. He held out his hand for reasons he did not understand as if he was expecting someone to take it and guide him. And then in the low tone of intrigue he asked her if it was true. Can you control the weather?

The girl shook her head.

"Are you sure?" he asked.

The moment gathered a seriousness that none of them expected. Even Burdean had been struck with curiosity and he stood frozen and waiting on her to clarify. The girl only stared back at Keal with her dark and unwavering eyes and she appeared to be at perfect ease in the suspension. Even the morning seemed to be silenced in anticipation of how the child would answer this time. No wind. No birdsong. The breathless hold of nature.

She didn't respond. She only traced her finger around her birthmark.

The girl then looked at Cara and she let go of her hand and walked back inside the house. Keal stood up straight and rested his hands on top of his head. None of them could think of what to say. They looked at the ground. Into the trees. Across the land where the smoke was dissipating like some forlorn memory. They looked anywhere but at each other. There was the flick of a lighter with Burdean lighting another cigarette. The gentle pat of Cara's steps as she began to pace around with her arms folded. Keal stared at the house but what he really saw was the image of the girl, waking and finding her standing in the window of the old hotel hideout with her body in a tremor and her hands balled into fists and the sky turned from clear to rolling with black clouds in the minutes in which he had fallen asleep.

"Hey," Burdean said to Cara. "You got a phone?"

"In the kitchen."

"Not like that."

"I had one but the signal was always for shit so I got rid of it."

"Good."

Burdean then reached into his pocket and he took out his

cell. He dropped it on the ground and stomped it and then he picked it up and threw it across the road and into the ditch.

"What about your phone?" Cara said to Keal.

"He's a purist like you," Burdean answered.

Burdean propped his hands on his hips. Cara crossed her arms.

"How come she won't answer us straight?" Keal said. And then the three of them milled around in their own muted interpretations of the girl's reticence. The tall tale that kept growing taller. The blue of dawn was at its end as the yellow sun came full over the horizon, but even in its rising glory it could not abate their darkness.

37

Keal walked over to the car and opened the door. He fished out the pocket watch and then returned to Burdean and Cara. They stood there suffering the long drain of silence and then finally Burdean said there's one surefire way to find out if it's real. Make her do it.

"You're kidding. Right?" Cara said.

"She either can or she can't."

"Do you really want to call her out here and tell her to make it rain or make the wind blow?"

"Yeah. I do."

"Have you not seen what she's been through? What her head is filled with?"

"I've seen enough to know that nobody can do what you just told us she can do."

"I didn't say she can do it. I said that's what they tell her she can do."

"Same thing."

Burdean tossed his cigarette and he looked at Keal who appeared hypnotized as he gazed through the window at the girl.

"Hey," he said. When Keal didn't answer he walked over to him and grabbed his shoulder. "Where's the pistol?"

Keal's head moved in a little shake. He stammered but then he said it's right here and he reached into the back of his pants and lifted it from his beltline.

"I'm going to town," Burdean said. "I'm putting gas in the car and getting more cigarettes and when I come back we're going to Ed's camp unless you don't want to and that goes for the both of you. But taking her there beats the hell out of sitting here where we clearly are not a secret. While I'm gone you sit out here by the front door with the pistol and shoot anything that moves. You understand?"

"Yeah."

"Do you?"

"I said yeah."

"Don't start daydreaming, Keal."

"What does that mean?"

"It means I know what you're thinking. That girl in there can't whip up a storm any more than I can."

"No shit."

"Yeah. No shit. You let your imagination run with this and it's only going to get harder and harder."

"To do what?"

"Anything."

38

Holygoddamnshit, Burdean thought. It feels good to be alone. He drove with the window down and no radio and the cool rush of the morning air. He felt the intensity drain from him the further away he got from the girl and the house and all of it, his body and his mind unclenching in small but noticeable increments. The big car wound through the hills, moving between shadow and light. The road rough and narrow. The blaze of autumn hanging in the trees in its last grim grasps of color. He felt a deliverance in his solitude though he knew it was temporary and he believed if he could have anything on this earth then it would be to keep driving until he came to the end of it.

He did just what he said he was going to do. He stopped at a convenience store and filled the car with gas and then he bought a carton of cigarettes. He did all this with attentive eyes. Unsure and suspecting of anyone and anything. A grandmother buying a lottery ticket. A teenage girl standing at the candy aisle. A bald man stocking the shelves with bags of potato chips. They all looked like killers to him.

When he was done he cranked the car and pulled around to the side of the store. A pay phone hung on the wall. He sat in the car and stared at it as if he was waiting for it to ring. And he wished it would. He wanted it to ring and he wanted to answer it and he wanted a voice of reason on the other end to explain all of this to him and then tell him what to do and then he wanted to go and do it and then everybody could go home.

He got out of the car. He dropped a quarter in the pay phone and he started to dial and then he hung up. The quarter dropped and rattled in the return slot and he picked it out. He walked out across the parking lot a few steps pulling at his ear and pulling at his beard and then he returned to the phone. He dropped the quarter in again and he dialed two numbers and then he hung up. The quarter dropped and he picked it out again and then he went back inside the store and poured a cup of coffee. He set it down on the register and held out two dollars to the woman sitting behind the counter. Her glasses rested on the end of her nose and when she rose from the stool she regarded him blackly. She did not speak and did not reach for the money.

"What?" he said.

"Nothing. Just wondering."

Burdean looked at her. Looked around as if someone else might help push her words from her mouth. He waved the two bills in front of her face to encourage her.

"Wondering what."

When Burdean lowered his hand she took the cash from him.

"I'm wondering what it is you're wrestling with out there by the phone."

"I ain't wrestling with nothing."

"That ain't what it looks like from here."

"Then you might try sliding your glasses up so you can see better."

"Don't matter."

"How come?"

"These glasses are for up close for reading."

"I don't see you reading nothing."

"I ain't currently."

"Then find something and quit watching me."

He walked back out and stood next to the pay phone, leaning against the brick wall and sipping the coffee and telling himself that there was him and only him and nothing else. He drank half the coffee and then tossed the other half out with a steamy splash on the concrete. He then pulled the quarter from his pocket and dropped it into the phone and he dialed again. When there was an answer he said I have her. I'll take the deal. Tell me when and where.

39

K eal moved the chair outside the front door and he did
like Burdean said. He sat there with the pistol in his
hand and he kept watch. But his mind had dived off
into the expanse of imagination with the suggestion of what this
child might be capable of doing. It triggered him back into his
childhood and the moment he came to believe in his own special powers of intuition. His own ability not to manipulate the
world, but to see its workings appear in the dreamscape and to
anticipate the turn of a moment or a sentence spoken or some
impending sorrow. He didn't believe she was a weather goddess
but he believed there was a damn good reason such an idea could
even come to life.

As a teenager he had seen his mother's sickness in the form
of a spreading mold. As a young man he had committed to never
sleeping again and he had managed it for years. As an outlaw
the dreams had returned and he had the premonition of an old

woman wandering through the darkness and then they had been approached by an old woman wandering through the darkness. He had been in a quarrel with the conscious and subconscious for his entire life and he both detested and craved sleep and there was a solitude in never being able to explain to anyone how the dreams and intuitions emerged or carried into the world and he recognized that solitude in the girl's eyes when he leaned closer and asked her if it was true. Can you do it? There was a depth in her stare that he had seen in the mirror a thousand times and it struck him that maybe in some other time or place he had already known her.

The front door was open and he looked over his shoulder. He could see down the short hallway and into the bathroom. The girl and Cara stood at the sink and took turns brushing their hair and washing their faces. The girl then sat down on the sofa. The angel drawing next to her. Cara went into the kitchen. Keal watched the road again and listened to the grind of broken glass underneath her feet when Cara moved across the floor and the snaps of bacon frying in a castiron skillet. Cara delivered a plate of bacon and toast to the girl and then she came outside, a cup of coffee in each hand. Keal took the offering and she sat down on the stoop next to the watchful chair.

His heightened curiosity about the girl had energized him and now he wanted to be brave with Cara. He wanted to ask her about the pills she took to sleep and why she wasn't running away screaming and what she was really doing here committed to this lunacy and why her house was so sparse and what her name was. But she was the one who started talking.

"Do you think it's possible we can see the same things in our heads?" she said.

"We like all of us or we like me and you."

"Like me and you. Not general stuff. Not common knowledge. But specifics. Things and people coming and going."

She did not look at him but she stared across the road. Out across the countryside that was bathed in the morning sun. A low mist blanketing the rolling hills. She looked different. Her face fresh and clean. Her eyes that became hawkish when she was serious and on-guard had softened into something gentle.

"I don't see why not. I'm beginning to believe just about anything," he answered.

"What do you believe right now? Tell me."

He sipped his coffee. Set the pistol down between his feet.

"I believe there's a chance that you'll believe me when I tell you I've always had particular dreams," he said. "Not like I'm a superhero or having dinner with famous people. Like intuitions. Maybe even forewarnings. Things you see happen and then they happen. I know it sounds made up but it's real."

"Why would I think it's made up?"

"I don't know. I just always figured people would."

"People probably would. But I don't."

They sat there in silence for a moment. Keal feeling like there was something seeping into him as she sat there with her questions and her answers and he liked hearing both of them. He had never had the chance to explain it to anyone else so he kept going.

"It started when I was a kid and went on for a long time. But then when I got older I tried to make it stop."

"How do you make it stop?"

"The only way I could figure was to quit sleeping. So I did. For a few years. Or I stopped as best I could. That seemed to take care of the dreams though it pretty much wrecked me for sleeping right ever again. But it finally came back. I started dreaming about a woman in the woods weeks ago. Maybe months. Over and over. And then there she was."

"Then I think we see the same things."

"Why is that?"

"Because two nights ago I was walking all around this house and I knew something was wrong with Wanetah. I knew she was somewhere she wasn't supposed to be. I can't say I dreamed it like you did but I knew she was out there like I know there is skin on my bones."

He looked at her. He wanted to ask if she was serious but he could see that she was.

"What else have you dreamed?"

He saw the storms and the lightning and the blaze of the treetops and the building that he had now seen twice. But he did not say it. Almost like if he admitted or described it, the dream would go away and he didn't want it to go away because he knew it was coming and he had to watch.

"Nothing," he said. "I haven't been asleep long enough."

She turned her head to him then. That's not true because I was standing there when it happened, she wanted to say. I was standing in the room and talking to you when you began to twitch and then you shrieked and jumped like something was after you. I saw you dreaming, she wanted to say. But that would have been confessing that she had moved close and she wasn't going to do that. Instead she raised her coffee cup to her mouth and he noticed her crooked fingers like he had noticed them many times before.

"Can I ask you what happened to your fingers?" he said.

"Yes."

"What happened to your fingers?"

The girl surprised them both when she stepped out of the door and stepped between them and walked out into the yard. She stopped at the mailbox and studied the black lump of burned possum in the middle of the road.

"If she touches that thing and it comes to life I swear to God I'm gonna take off running," Keal said.

"They didn't say she was Jesus."

"A miracle is a miracle as far as I'm concerned. Don't matter if it's raising the dead or whipping up a tornado."

The sound of an engine grumbled from down the road. Keal picked up the pistol but as the grumbling came closer Cara told him to put it down. That's just Billy. As the vehicle approached a rattling combined with the grumbling and when the old truck passed Billy waved, a trailer loaded with lawnmowers and leafblowers and weedeaters rattling behind him.

The girl then leaned against the mailbox and she pointed her finger and made a drawing motion.

"She does that a lot," Keal said. "Traces with her finger. She does it to her birthmark. She does it to the angel. She's done it like that in the air a few times."

They watched her as she weaved her finger, seeing something that only she could see. Then she noticed she was being watched and she lowered her hand and she walked back toward the house. She passed them and went inside and sat down on the sofa. Keal asked Cara if she had something to write with and write on and Cara set her coffee cup on the step and went into the kitchen and returned to the porch with a notebook and a pencil. Keal set the pistol in the chair seat and he took the notebook and pencil from her and then he went inside to the girl.

"If you like to draw, here you go," he said.

She took it. Her dark eyes seemed to lighten and she nodded. Keal returned to Cara outside.

"What do you want her to draw?" she said.

"I don't care. I figure whatever it is, maybe it'll be some kind of clue as to what's in that little brain."

"I don't think that's a little brain."

"What kind of brain do you think it is?"

"I think it's the kind of brain that neither me or you can grasp."

Keal grabbed the pistol from the chair seat and sat back down. Cara picked up her coffee but remained standing. She sipped and snuck a glance at the girl who had opened the notebook.

"So what happened to your fingers?" Keal said.

She held out her hand toward him. She had never bothered to hide them but she had never exposed them so freely to another. She had performed this motion alone so many times but now she felt an unanticipated liberation in putting them on display.

"You made yourself stop sleeping," she said. "Somebody else made me."

She lowered her fingers. Keal set the pistol down again. He looked around the scalded landscape. The azaleas black and sickly. The widereaching spread of charred ground.

"You believe he's coming back?" Cara asked.

"Who?"

"Your buddy."

"I do. I do think so."

"You trust him."

"I've never had a reason not to."

"That don't always matter."

Cara walked into the yard. Strolling as if this was some casual and coolweathered day meant for them to enjoy. The singsong of birds filled the air and though there was the sun and the sky and a picture that suggested that it was possible for the world to be beautiful, all she could think about was later when the light would fade and she would sink into melancholy. She walked a half circle and returned and stopped in front of Keal.

"Can I ask you a question?"

"If you want."

"There is a special kind of loneliness that comes from not being able to sleep. I've come to understand that. A loneliness like no other I have found and I've found a few. Do you understand this?"

He nodded and now he was in it with another person as if a secret he had been carrying his entire life had been exposed. He understood that loneliness with depth and clarity. It was a place from which you cannot escape and you are left to lie there in the black silence of your solitude. You can almost believe you have been delivered to a mindweary purgatory where you are one benevolent step away from the sleep of heaven but you cannot repent or be forgiven of the sins that keep you awake. Sometimes you lie there and believe you are the only one who suffers. But all of the time you are alone.

Keal stood from the chair. Something knocked loose inside of him.

"Do you want to leave?" she said.

"Leave where?"

"Here. We can get in my car and we can leave."

She reached into the front pocket of her jeans and pulled out the rolls of cash she had kept from Wanetah.

"We can get pretty far away."

"You said you didn't want to leave."

"I didn't mean it that way. I meant I didn't want to leave with your friend. I don't trust him like you do."

Yes, he wanted to say. We can leave. It seemed the most simple thing. But it was not a simple thing. He reached out and touched the money with the tip of his finger and imagined it rolling across the ground in the firelight in the moment that the old woman appeared and the instant it took for him to figure out if she was real or in his head.

"That money is following me around," he said.

"Do you want to?"

"I'm not running off on him. We've all been damn near killed and that's reason enough for me to want to hold together. Besides he knows people and places I don't know that probably matter."

"Matter to what?"

"To staying alive. To keeping that girl alive or getting her wherever she needs to be or a bunch of other things I'm sure I'm not considering."

"Then maybe we don't see the same things," she said.

"Why is that?"

"Because. I see something in him that you don't."

He did not know if she was wrong or if she was right but he wanted to keep talking to her. There was a language between them he didn't know existed. He took a step toward her and there were only questions in his mind but he did not get to ask any more of them as the sound of the car interrupted the country quiet. Keal snatched the pistol from beneath the chair and Cara rushed inside to the girl and Keal stood with the pistol gripped and ready. But it was only Burdean. The big car turned into the drive and pulled up next to the house and through the open window Burdean said I thought I told you to shoot at anything that moves.

40

Keal called to Cara and the girl and told them it was all right. Burdean got out of the car and Keal met him at the cracked headlight.

"We'll go to the camp this evening," Burdean said.

"What happened to when I get back I'm taking the girl and I'm going to the camp and you can go or not and all that big talk?"

"I don't know, Keal. What happens to anything."

"Going to the camp is fine but what happens after?"

"After what?"

"We go to the camp and live happily ever after?"

Burdean moved his eyes from Keal. He rubbed at his wounded shoulder.

"I wouldn't worry about it," he said.

"Wouldn't worry about it?"

"That's what I said."

"What does that mean?"

Burdean walked past him and over to the chair. He looked down and saw the coffee cup and then he went inside the house. Through the broken windows Keal heard him ask Cara if there was more coffee and there was. He returned holding a cup and then he told Keal that he had called a guy who might be able to help.

"Help how?"

"He might know something."

"Could you be any more vague?"

"Okay. Fine. I called a guy who says he can't talk about it on the phone but he knows more about the girl and about the crowd of people looking for her. He told me to meet him back at the truckstop tonight and he'd fill me in. We'll do that and then we'll go to the camp and maybe we'll have some info that'll help us figure out what's next. That better?"

"It ain't worse."

Keal watched him smoking and drinking coffee. Thinking that Burdean seemed bothered and Cara's words crossed his mind. I see something in him that you don't.

"We could simplify this," Keal said.

"How so?"

"We can drop the girl off at the front door of the sheriff's department and keep going," Keal said. He didn't mean it but he wanted to see how Burdean would react.

Burdean didn't answer. He walked around in a short circle.

"Or the police station either one. Or the hospital. Or the mayor's office or the post office or anydamnwhere. Just drop her off. She won't say nothing because she don't know nothing to say. She don't know our names. She might not even talk at all without the woman around."

Burdean smoked.

"The woman in there don't know nothing to say either. We can take the kid and go. Be somewhere pretty far gone by night."

Burdean flicked away his cigarette.

"Give me the pistol," he said.

Keal held the gun in his hand but he didn't pass it over. The men looked at one another. Then Burdean held out his hand to confirm the request but Keal didn't move.

"What's happening here, Keal?"

"Nothing."

"You and her have a little powwow while I was gone?"

"No."

"You sure?"

"I'm sure if you're sure."

"If I'm sure about what?"

"About where you went and who you talked to."

Burdean withdrew his hand. He studied Keal and then he backed up a few steps and leaned against the car. He finished the coffee and set the cup on the hood and he saw Cara watching them from the front room. Then he walked around to the driver's side and he reached inside the open window and pulled the keys from the ignition. He came back to Keal and pitched the keys to him and Keal snatched them out of the air. He then took his two rolls of cash from his coat pocket and he tossed them on the ground at Keal's feet.

"Do what you want," he said.

"I didn't mean it like that."

"You got the gun. You got the keys. You got the money. You want to drop the miracle worker off with the cops, go ahead. You want to drive off and leave me standing here, go ahead. You want to shoot me, go ahead."

Keal knelt and picked up the two rolls. He stepped over to Burdean and he handed them over along with the pistol and the keys. Burdean then set it all on the roof of the car.

"Later when it starts to get dark we'll go and do what I said we were gonna do. You change your mind before then, there it all is right there on top of the car. I ain't gonna touch none of it. Fair?"

"Fair," Keal said.

The front door opened and Cara came out. She stepped between the men and she lifted the pistol from the car roof and said if the bad guys show up I'll give this back but neither one of you need to put your fingers on it until then. She stomped back inside and then the girl came out. She walked over to Keal and handed him what she had drawn. It was a circle and inside the circle were four stick figures. Above the stick figures there was a cloud. Reaching from the cloud and striking the circle was a lightning bolt.

DUSK

41

The four of them loaded into the big car. Burdean drove. Keal in the front. Cara and the girl in the backseat. When the girl climbed in she handed Keal the framed angel to hold while she opened up the notebook and began to draw in the waning light. Keal set the frame on the floorboard between him and Burdean. The car moved through the country in the hour of transformation, a thick silence between its passengers. They moved along the hills and then came to the highway. Headlights greeted them. A reminder that there were lives less threatened in the movement of the passing vehicles. After a handful of miles Cara reached over the seat and handed the pistol back to Burdean. It was passed and taken without a word and as the car descended the final hill and the world flattened, the last of the smokey light sunk into the swamplands and disappeared into the dark water as if earth and sky had joined together as one.

The road was straight and empty. A matte black sky in a nightfall cloud cover. If not for the knowledge that they were headed in the right direction it might have been a road to nowhere but each mile through the lowlands brought them closer to some idea of an answer. But that idea was unspoken and different behind each set of eyes that stared out of the car windows. Immersed in their own dark and their own makings of where this was going.

The solitary lights of the truckstop appeared ahead but the car did not slow down. Keal sat up in his seat thinking that Burdean's mind was somewhere else and he said there it is. But Burdean did not slow then either and the car went right past.

"I thought that's where you said we were going," Keal said.

"Not right now. We're going a little further."

"To do what."

"Just ride."

"Bullshit. What the hell are we doing?"

Burdean raised the pistol and tapped the muzzle on the dash.

"I said just ride. You had your chance."

A new air filled the space between them. The hardness of doubt. Keal glanced over his shoulder at Cara who met his eyes with the same worry. Burdean drove on and the lights of the truckstop disappeared behind them.

"Don't," Keal said.

"Don't what."

"Whatever this is."

"Stop talking."

Burdean sat fixed in resignation and he held the pistol in a firm grip. He nestled the steering wheel with his knees and with his other hand he rolled the window down an inch and reached for his cigarettes and when he did he noticed the frame with the drawing of the angel on the floorboard. He picked it up and held it in the glow of the dashlight and he wanted it to be gone. He wanted everything and everybody they had run across since they had sat around the fire in the woods to be gone and it all would be soon enough. Each thump of the road was a thump closer to his own preservation and he felt it like a heartbeat. He raised the frame to the crack in the window to slide it out into the night but then he was reminded what Keal had said about it. The girl seems to like it. He fought back his surging animosity and instead of pushing it out of the window he handed it back over the seat to the girl. She took it from him.

"Thank you," she said.

Burdean looked over at Keal. And then he turned and looked back at the girl and the three adults shot their eyes back and forth at one another in the surprise of her response while she sat docile and gazing at the drawing. Burdean drove on but he couldn't help watching the girl in the rearview mirror, wondering if she had anything else to say and when she turned her attention from the drawing and stared back at him in the mirror he became agitated. Shifting in his seat. A gnawing inside as the girl kept watching him in the mirror with her dark and consuming eyes but he drove on.

A few more miles and the car slowed. A cinderblock bar sat off the road in a glob of yellowgreen light. The bar backed up to the marsh and a mist crept out of the swamp and reached over the roof and across the gravel and across the road. An SUV was parked at one end of the bar and there was no sign of life. No music. No lights shining from behind the two grimy windows. No movement but for the insects dancing in the sickly neon sign that hung on the end of the building and read simply BAR. Their car rolled across the gravel and came to a stop. There was a singular door in the offset center of the building, metal and windowless and dented from the beating of trying to get in or trying to get out.

Burdean killed the ignition and stuck the keys in his coat pocket.

"What in God's name?" Keal said.

"I agree with him," Cara said.

Burdean lit a cigarette. He looked again into the rearview mirror and the girl was staring at him.

"You need to fess up," Keal said.

"And you need to shut up."

Burdean got out of the car. He smoked and looked around and there was no light and no semblance of anything in any direction. The swamp trees stood naked against the coming winter. Bats darted through the dark in spasms of hunt. Silent lightning flashed in the distant sky behind a widereaching curtain of nightclouds.

Burdean slipped the pistol into his coat pocket but he kept his hand on it. He then took four steps toward the door and he stopped. Debating. He returned and opened the car door and handed the keys to Keal.

"If you drive off and leave me again I will find you and kill you and I hope you can look at me right now and see that I mean it."

"I won't."

"Just the same if things go bad or feel bad then get the hell out of here."

"How am I supposed to know the difference?"

"You will."

Burdean shut the door. The dusk had slipped into pure black space and he looked up into the great expanse as if there was an answer gathering itself somewhere in the beyond. He then lowered his eyes and stole one more glance at the girl and she met his eyes. He walked back to the bar and stood at the metal door and he dropped his head and whispered to himself as if saying a prayer of resolve or maybe forgiveness and then he opened the door.

42

A mostly empty room. Soursmelling and soaked in dread. Burdean held the door open and the yellowgreen neon fell into the room. He stood in the threshold and tried to see what he could see. A pool table with a cue and a few striped balls. A scattering of folding chairs, some upright and some turned on their side. A concrete floor and a makeshift bar made out of bowed plywood and empty dustcovered bottles gathered in a bunch at the end of the bar. Everything coated with the layer of grime from time forgotten and foretold. He tried to imagine that once there had been lights and liquor and a jukebox and maybe even a good time but he only felt the impression that this place was the hovel for men a couple of grades worse than he was. He held the door open and he lifted the pistol from his coat pocket and he was a halfthought away from backing out when there was a click. Lamplight appeared in the corner of the bar where two men sat next to a stack of empty crates.

"Close the door," one of them said.

He closed the door.

"Put it on the pool table."

"Nope."

"Put it on the pool table or you won't leave here."

Burdean stepped to the pool table and laid the pistol next to the cue.

"And the coat."

"Why you want me to take off my coat?"

"Why don't you want to?"

Burdean removed his coat and laid it in a wad next to the table. There was a bloodspot on his shirt where he had bled through the bandage.

"Step away."

Burdean did as he was told. He looked over at the men and they were little more than shadow in the bald light.

"Do you have the girl?"

"Do you have the money?"

The men stood. One of them picked up the lamp and carried it with him as they came toward Burdean, an extension cord dragging across the floor behind the lamp and smacks in their footsteps as their feet stuck to the tacky floor. As they approached their features became more evident and when he laid eyes on the one who was doing the talking he lost the reason why he was here as the man looked too much like him. The same graying beard and the same lines in the weary eyes and the same blue-collar build and it caused him to take a step back, hit with the notion that he was the subject of a mimicry. A fooling about. Mired in a dreamwash of a story he did not want to be told. The difference was a scar that stretched across the width of the man's forehead and Burdean touched his fingers to his own forehead as if to make sure he did not have the same scar and when he did not feel it he believed it was coming. He looked at the other man. He had a sunken jaw and the sleepyeyed tranquility of the halfdead and his fingers were wrapped around the neck of the lamp, his fingernails rimmed in dirtbrown.

"Where is she?" the man said.

The words shook Burdean back into focus. He heard the man but he wanted to hear him again.

"What?"

"I said where is she?"

"You are not who I talked to on the phone. You are not the voice. Where is he?"

"Where is who?"

"The wiry and weird looking guy with the Elvis sideburns."

"I'm not sure what you mean."

"The voice."

"Not that. Who is this other fellow you mentioned? This Elvis guy."

The man gave him a smirk.

"We're all pretty far gone in this godforsaken place. But we ain't that far gone," Burdean said.

"That's good to know. But this voice you're talking about. It doesn't matter."

"It does."

The man holding the lamp moved to the pool table and propped his hip against it. He set the lamp on the table next to Burdean's pistol. He then took out a knife and opened the blade and he began to pick at his dirty nails. The man with the scar then lifted a tumbled chair and he sat down. The two men moved as if they were actors in a play, rehearsed in their movements and knowing what was going to be said and how to respond and perfectly content in the pace of the tale.

"Just because I am not the voice you heard on the telephone, it doesn't mean I am not the voice," the man said. "We are all the voice. We are all together. You. Me and him. The ones sitting in your car outside. The ones asleep in their beds. The ones moving about in places near and far, doing whatever it is that they do. You cannot separate it."

"That's all fine and dandy. Except that this is a simple thing we're supposed to be doing."

The man with the dirty fingernails laughed. He did not look up from his attention to the knife and nails but he kept laughing until the other man shushed him.

"Hush," he said. "He can't help it. He don't know any better."

"I know plenty," Burdean said. And he stood there waiting for the man to say something else but both of them were quiet. The man with the scar relaxed in the chair and crossed his legs. The man with the knife held up his hand to see how the cleaning was going.

A flash of light appeared in the windows. Another vehicle pulling into the parking lot. Burdean turned and saw it stop next to the big car and then the headlights shut off. Blacked out windows. Neither of the men gave it their attention but what Burdean could not see was the attention that Keal and Cara were giving it, Keal climbing behind the wheel and slipping the key in the ignition and Cara telling the girl to get down and the girl lying across the floorboard in the backseat with Cara leaning over her to hide her and protect her from whatever was coming.

"What do you want?" Burdean said.

The man with the knife laughed again.

"That funny?"

"What do we want?" the man with the scar said.

"That's right."

"You're the one who called us."

Burdean then understood he was talking to himself. He was asking questions that were not going to get an answer and he was asking them to his own scarred self-image and the moment and the murkiness and the riddle of it all felt like a trial for some wrongdoing that would not be explained to him. A trial whose verdict had already been determined. He believed this night had already occurred. How many times he did not know but he was filled with the certainty that he had been here before with these men in this dingy light at the end of these mystifying days that had shown him a world that lingered on the outskirts of everything he thought he knew. He watched the man with the knife and thought of those dirty fingernails and those dirty hands being placed on the girl and he heard her small voice tell him thank you when he handed her the drawing and he knew then that indifference would only carry you so far through this life before it left you in the stranglehold of regret.

"You mind if I smoke?" he said.

The man with the scar shrugged. Burdean reached into his shirt pocket and took out cigarettes and a lighter. He tapped one out and lit it and then he held out the pack to offer but neither acknowledged him.

"You mind if I sit down?"

He didn't wait for an answer. He crossed the floor and picked up a chair and he returned to the spot where he had been standing and he set the chair down and sat. Facing his own image. They even sat the same way. Leaned back. Arm draped over the chairback. Lazy in posture but grave across the eyes.

Drink and fight and fuck, Burdean thought. What a nice and simple life it had been. But it was over. And it had been over since the moment he thought to pick up the phone and make a deal. He sat and smoked and reveled in how far down the road he had been able to make it sustained by those three abilities and the men let him be as if understanding the realizations he was making about his life. By the end of the cigarette Burdean had shifted from the satisfaction of those years to the lamentation of loss for all he had known. But he did not wallow because he figured there were decisions yet to be made.

"I'm curious about something," he said.

The man with the scar nodded. Burdean sat up straight. Leaned forward with his elbows resting on his knees.

"Where did you come from?" he said.

The men looked at each other.

"Where did you and him and all this come from? Huh? Everything that's going on with this big hunt. This story about the girl. Where did it come from?"

"Story?"

"Yeah. Story. All this cockamamie bullshit if you want the truth about it all."

"The truth?"

"Are you a goddamn echo?"

Burdean tapped out another cigarette and lit it.

"Stuff like this is made up to fill pockets. That's all it is."

"Stuff like what exactly?"

"You know what. That she can control the weather. Whip

up a storm or make it snow. Sounds straight from the Old Testament and those kind of tales have been known to drum up a dollar or two."

"You mean like you are doing," the man said. "You are here to drum up a dollar or two. I cannot think of another reason you would put yourself in this situation."

"I suppose," Burdean said. He leaned back in the chair again. "I can't really argue that. But that don't answer what I asked. It don't explain what's on your end. Who is the voice?"

"A better way to put it may be what is the voice. Do you believe that the world turns on its own?"

"I can't say I've thought much about it."

The man with the scar stood from the chair and he strolled over to Burdean.

"You look like somebody I know," he said.

"Yeah. Who's that?"

The man smiled.

"It's something. You and me. I wonder if there is a third we haven't met."

"Where's my money?"

The man with the scar sighed as if disappointed.

"There are greater things," he said.

The man with the knife stood from the pool table. He looked at his gross nails as if he had somehow improved them. But he didn't close the blade. He walked over to the window and looked out at the big car and the car beside it and then he turned and nodded and Burdean could feel it coming. The scar across his forehead and the girl gone and whatever bad end that was coming to Keal and Cara and he had about a second to figure out how to rectify the choice he had made when the man with the scar backed away from him and sat down again in the chair.

"Your money is in the cellar," he said.

"What cellar?"

"You know what cellar."

"I ain't going back there. I ain't going nowhere children are hid in the pitch black dark like an animal. Worse than an animal."

"She's not a child. I thought you understood that. And she wasn't hidden. She can never be hidden. She is always where she is supposed to be. Like you. Like me."

"I don't give a shit what she is or where she is or about any of your crackpot philosophy. I ain't going back there."

"You are if you want what was promised."

"What the hell is wrong with you and everybody else?"

"It's just poetry, Burdean. Grim poetry."

He did not like it when the man said his name. And then it struck him this was likely the last time he would hear another person speak it. He smoked and tried to calm himself. He looked around the forgotten barroom and he envisioned a redheaded bartender with long eyelashes wearing a tanktop and possessing the curves of the bottle she was pouring from, looking up at him and smiling that smile that tells you everything you need to know about what is going to happen before the night is over. He almost smiled himself as memories of such nights caused his expression to ease. His demeanor transitioning from the angst of the moment into the acceptance of it.

"I don't believe you about the money," he said.

"I understand."

"But I don't guess I have a choice."

"That's all we have. Until we don't."

The man with the knife crossed the floor, moving behind Burdean. Burdean eased up from the chair and turned his shoulders to where he could see them both and he took a long drag on the cigarette. A long and serene drag of goodbye. He then exhaled, blowing a final smoke ring, an impressive smoke ring that floated into the air and held in a loose circle between the two men, who were caught in their admiration of it when Burdean flicked the cigarette at the man with the knife and darted for the pistol on the pool table. He snatched it and turned and fired as the man with the knife came for him with the blade raised and Burdean missed and the blade sunk into his gunshot shoulder. He screamed but stuck the pistol in the man's stomach and fired again, a guttural blow that took the strength from the knife handle and he and Burdean fell back across the pool table. Burdean's pistol hand was caught beneath the man's weight but he fired again into his stomach and the man slid off, Burdean wrestling to get out from under him but he could not get free before the man with the scar got there and pulled the blade from his shoulder and then just as Burdean rolled the dead man aside the blade came down through his ribcage in the instant that his hand came free and he fired and the bullet split the scar across the man's forehead.

The man dropped straight down as if falling into a hole. Outside car engines cranked with the sound of gunshots as Burdean lay on the pool table bleeding hard and fast with the blade lodged in his ribs. There was the sound of spinning gravel and then the sound of metal slamming against metal and then engines revved again and metal crashed again and then the concussion of the building being rocked with collision, the cinderblock wall cracking and bending. Burdean dropped his head back on the green felt. His hand on the handle of the blade. Staggered breaths and a darkening world and he tried to find the strength to pull the blade from his ribs but he could not and his arms fell to his sides.

The door opened and Keal ran inside and between his holy shits and oh fucks he pulled the blade from Burdean who let out an agonizing groan and bloodspit came from the corners of his mouth. Keal tossed the blade away and he picked up the pistol from the floor and then he managed to raise him, getting Burdean's arm draped around his neck and he carried him outside. The big car had smashed the other car and then rammed it into the side of the building, pinning it to where no one could get out but it did not seem to matter as one head lay facedown on the dashboard and another was snapped back over the headrest. Cara had hopped the seat and was behind the wheel with the girl next to her and Keal opened the back door. Burdean flopped across the backseat and then Keal climbed in and Cara shifted into reverse, stomped the gas, rocks and dust spitting out from underneath the spinning tires. Smoke rose from the engine and when she shifted into drive the transmission missed but then caught and as they hit pavement and sped away Keal told Burdean it's a good damn thing you drive a car the size of a tank.

43

Take me to my room. Take me to my room. Burdean kept saying the same thing when they wanted to stop and try and get him some help. Don't stop. Take me to my room. His labored breathing and the drain of his voice. Keal had taken off his coat and held it pressed against Burdean's wounds, Burdean slumped across the backseat and his head against the window and his eyes looking out at nothing. The girl got on her knees and turned around in the seat and she laid her hand on Burdean's forearm. Take me to my room he kept saying so that's what they did.

Cara parked in the alleyway next to the old hotel. Keal managed to get Burdean out of the big car and up the metal grate stairway. By the time they made it upstairs and to the end of the hallway they were both covered in Burdean's blood. The deadbolt held the door closed and locked and the key was on the key ring that hung from the ignition but it was gone. After Keal had lifted Burdean out of the car, Cara said I'm going to get something or somebody and she and the girl drove off in search of help. Keal cussed when he saw the deadbolt and he could figure only one way into the room. He removed Burdean's arm from around his neck and he lowered him to the floor, propping his back against the wall. Music bumped from down the hallway and goodtiming voices and the aggravated shouts from other rooms threatening them if they didn't shut the hell up joined together and made big noise and it drowned out the wham wham wham of Keal kicking at the door. Splintering and then busting the frame where the padlock held and he tore it away. Burdean sagged against the wall and Keal slid his hands under his arms and dragged him into the room.

He propped Burdean on the bed, reclined on a couple of flimsy pillows. And then he didn't know what to do. He tried talking and telling Burdean to hold on. It's going to be okay just hold on. But he didn't believe it and neither did Burdean who lay there gashed and dying and when Keal kept going with the promises of salvation yet to come, Burdean couldn't take it anymore.

"Stop," he said.

Keal stood next to the bed. He nodded.

"Money," Burdean said. "My coat. Go get it."

"What money?"

"The two rolls. The old woman. It's back there."

"I don't care."

"Go back. Get it. Keep going."

"Burdean. Damn it. Just hold on."

Burdean raised his hand. Lathered in his blood.

"Maybe she can help," he said. His voice fading.

"Who can? Help with what?"

"The girl. The storms. Maybe she can help. Maybe she can keep us from all they say is coming our way."

Burdean then lowered his hand and laid it down by his side. He looked away from Keal and toward the darkness outside the window. And then he closed his eyes. Keal started talking again but he did not hear him. Keal's voice trailing away, moving off into a realm never to be heard again. And then the racket of the hallway began to fade and all fell into silence. In the world behind his eyes Burdean saw himself learning to drive. His father beside him and coaching him on the clutch and the gas pedal and the rhythm of shifting just right and how good it felt when the gears transitioned in smooth acceleration and then he saw himself driving without his father and he was filled with the great liberation of being alone. The great liberation of being alone that at times had pacified him while in other times it had caused him a great hunger and sent him searching for others. But then the feelings of youth and liberation and loneliness joined together and slipped away and he was gathered by a heavy warmth, carrying only one thought with him into the soundless and colorless void.

We are a part of the hand of God. And it is soaked in blood.

44

Keal was standing in the alley when the big car returned. Smoke seeping from the edges of the hood. A hissing and chugging from the engine. Cracks reached across the windshield like a spread of river veins. One headlight destroyed. A crushed grille.

He had taken off and tossed his coat. Blood smeared on his hands. Across his cheek. Wiped on his shirt and the thighs of his jeans. The pistol tucked into the front of his pants. Cara said something to the girl and then she got out holding a plastic bag that held gauze and patches and medical tape and whatever else she had grabbed in the rush of trying to do anything for Burdean. She only needed to look at Keal to understand what had happened. She stepped to the dumpster and tossed the plastic bag over the side.

Then she turned to him.

"What was his name?" she said.

"Burdean."

"What's your name?"

"Keal."

"Do you want to know mine?"

"I know it."

He had looked into a kitchen drawer and dug around and found a piece of mail with her name on it when he was looking for a photograph of her or anything that would tell him more about her sleepless life in the empty house. But he hadn't revealed her name to Burdean as part of their pact to remain anonymous and she didn't ask how he knew.

"What else do you know?"

He shook his head. A gloom fell over him. His hanging expression. His slack posture that barely kept him standing. She studied him and thought that he seemed to be slowly disappearing as someone might walk into a cloud. He then reached into his pocket and he pulled out the pocket watch. Somewhere was the violent man it belonged to. Somewhere were more faceless men who would come after the girl and there were more dreams he did not want to dream and more woods to be haunted and more old women to wander in confusion and more wolves in the night and more depths of things he could not understand and he felt the weight of everything that had happened and everything that was to come in the timehold of the broken watch. He snapped it shut and he turned and threw it high and far down the alley and it came apart nicely when it busted on the concrete and he wished there were more things he could pick up and throw and be rid of.

"I don't know anything," he said.

"She told me her name. Do you want to know it?"

Keal raised his eyes and looked at the girl through the splintered glass of the windshield.

"No."

He walked past Cara and to the car and he climbed into the backseat. Cara ran her eyes up the stairway. Ran her eyes along the second floor of the once grand hotel to the last window. Burdean's window. It was illuminated and she realized that Keal had been unable to leave him in the dark.

45

By the time they returned to Cara's house they had reached a decision. Keal was going back to the barroom to recover Burdean's coat with the two rolls of cash. Cara would pack up whatever she thought she and the girl needed and when Keal returned they would leave and go and disappear somewhere. If Keal wasn't back at the house by daybreak then something had met him along the way and she and the girl would get in the Volkswagen and flee alone.

Keal cleaned Burdean's blood from his face and hands and he slugged the remaining half bottle of wine. Cara walked about the house with her arms folded as if trying to remember something that she had no chance of remembering. The girl sat on the sofa with the framed angel on the cushion next to her and outside the clouds gathered in the grayblack sky and the lightning flashed in muted strikes and the winds carried it closer.

Keal walked out of the house and then he turned around and walked right back in. He went into the kitchen where the crucifix hung on the nail and he lifted it and hung the ribbon around his neck and tucked the broken relic inside his shirt in an act of desperation and then he was gone.

46

A halfmile away from the cinderblock bar Keal turned from the road and onto a risen strip of levee that weaved through the swampy terrain. He parked and he opened the door and sat there listening to the night. The theater of darkness played with caws and groans and croaks and he heard the random splash of predator and prey. Cypress knots poked up from the blackwater like arms reaching for deliverance and the drape of the willows reached down toward them as if nature on her own could join hands and save herself. The lightning danced behind boulders of clouds in sporadic quietude and Keal admired the tranquility he felt in the natural world even if it had been calamity that had delivered him to this moment.

In the shine of the remaining headlight he had seen a pathway that led from the levee and cut across the marshland and he raised from the car seat and started in the direction of the bar. Wanting to sneak up on it in case others had appeared. A deepening haze swallowed the yellowgreen neon, a murky and sickly beacon. In his mind there were alligators with great jaws and great hunger lying in wait along the pathway, their bulging eyes and ancient heads appearing as every fallen limb or clump of Spanish moss that lingered on the surface of the sodden world. It kept him moving quickly, the earth sucking at his feet and the lightning dancing above. He walked on fixated on the hazy neon and all seemed quiet and then he paused to knock the muddy clumps from his bootheels and when he did he noticed the silence. The pause of the life around him. And there was no more lightning but only the lungs of the dark.

A gentle and nearly soundless rain began to fall then and he recognized it the same way he always recognized the instant when his dreams appeared in front of him. With a halfsecond of astonishment that was followed by the intrigue of watching the premonition unfold. He had felt this rain and heard this silence and he knew what was coming next. He raised his face and palms to the sky and felt the cleansing and waited for the crash of thunder and then he heard it coming from miles away, rolling toward him in an avalanche of sound that ripped through both him and the earth. The rain disappeared and the rush of the wind came next, following the chronology. Pushing across the flatland in a wave of gusts and the thunder bellowed and joined with the wind in the sudden rush of power and Keal knew that at any instant it would all stop and return to silence and then it would be time to run.

He watched. It stopped.

A crack of lightning ruptured the night. And then another and another and Keal began running along the pathway, slipping and sinking and fighting against the soggy ground and then the lightning began to assault the landscape just as he had seen, the strikes into the treetops of cypresses and cottonwoods. Showers of spark and flame appearing against the dark in bursts of white and gold and he ran ducking and desperate for a cover that he knew would not be there because the dream was alive and in the dream there was no shelter and only the destruction of the building he was running toward but he ran on with no choice and with the hope that he could defeat the dream and he was coming closer and closer to the cinderblock bar and all he needed was a handful of seconds to run inside and grab the coat and run back out and let the lightning do its work to the decrepit roadside joint. He made it from the pathway and into the gravel of the parking lot and he saw the car smashed against the outer wall and he saw the dented metal door and he could see himself with the coat and money tucked under his arm as he raced back for the big car when the destruction that was promised in his dream occurred in a split second terror strike of lightning that exploded the roof of the building. Keal dropped and rolled in the gravel and covered his head as if he had been delivered onto some long ago battlefield where cannonballs crushed men and earth without mercy or prejudice.

He lay there covered up, listening to the lightning cracks and the echoes of the cracks that trailed off into the reaches of night and he expected to feel a fatal zap into his back at any instant and the satisfaction in leaving his body the instant after. That was not in his dream and he never died in his dream because he always woke when the building was struck so he kept his head down and he flinched with the sound of each bolt. But the strike into his back never came. And the lightning ceased. When he felt secure enough to raise his head from the gravel and

look around, the roof of the building was burning and break-
ing and collapsing. He hustled to his feet and over to the door.
He opened it and a beam had fallen across the pool table and
Burdean's coat smoldered and the dead men burned and as he
watched the flames he could not help but wonder if the girl had
been responsible for everything that he had seen both behind his
eyes and in front of them.

47

Two months after her fingers had been broken and other things had been broken, Cara was returning home after a visit to Wanetah, unable to shake the accumulation of clutter inside her house that was growing in accordance with the old woman's dementia and there was nothing that could be done to slow the spread of either one. She parked the Volkswagen and she went into her house, moving with the impulse of emptying her life in every way that she could empty it. The first thing she did was box up anything that belonged to her grandmother and she moved it into the attic. When the relics of sentiment were safe she then went from room to room with a garbage bag. She removed frames from the wall and cards and letters from drawers and books and keepsakes from shelves. She emptied clothes from the dresser and pulled shirts and dresses from hangers in the closet. She did not allow herself to pause when she came across something that triggered an emotion. She worked to rid the house of any sentiment and she came out of the house every few minutes with a full garbage bag and there were ten of them stacked by the road when she was done. Then she dragged out the pieces of pointless furniture and she set end tables and rugs and lamps beside the gathering of garbage bags and she realized it was collection day when she heard the garbage truck rolling down the road and she stood there in the yard and watched the man in the orange vest toss the bags and the furniture into the back of the truck as if she needed proof that it was all being carried away.

When the garbage truck drove off she climbed back in the Volkswagen and drove to the hardware store where she bought gallons of paint and brushes and rollers and a ladder and then she called and quit her job at the grocery store because there would always be another job where all they needed was a body and then she worked as a house painter every day until each room and the exterior of the house had been given a fresh coat. The work took weeks and kept her muscles sore but the movement helped to steady her thoughts and eradicate the image of the man standing in her yard in the middle of the night, waiting to hurt her as if he had been bought and paid for by someone who had reasons to hate her.

The purge satisfied her. A healing by subtraction. And when she lay awake and restless at night or walked around barefoot in the dewdamp grass or sat on the porch drinking from a bottle of red or a bottle of cold white, she worked to replace her melancholy with the belief that there would be a moment when her life would change and by living with such scarcity there would be no weight and if she needed to she could leave this place without a second thought. That moment had occurred with such ferocity that she could find no way to question its arrival.

There was nothing to gather for her and the girl. She did not have a suitcase or a travel bag and if she did there was nothing she wanted to take other than a toothbrush and underwear and socks which she had dropped into a pillowcase. She figured that wherever they were going, there would be stores that sold the things they needed. The man who had set the yard on fire had left a little gas in the gas can and she had poured it into the Volkswagen tank and other than that she could not think of one thing to do.

The girl lay asleep on the sofa. The house dark. Cara sat in a chair outside the front door and waited for Keal. The rolls of cash in her pocket. At sunup they would leave without him and sunup was drawing close. She thought about Wanetah and she wished she could see her again and hoped that somewhere in Wanetah's mind she held the image of the woman who would stop by and bring her food and sit and visit with her.

She could hear the storm coming in their direction. And she could smell the rain on the wind and then the thunder was right above and the wind gusted and the rain thrummed through the trees and then there came the cracks of lightning and she did not know why but she rose from the chair and she walked out across the yard, the wind and the rain on her face and the white light flashing around her but she was not scared and she reveled in the surge of the fastmoving storm. She stood with her arms outstretched until the rain passed on and then there was only the wind and the lightning and she looked back at the house as if to check for the girl's safety and when she did the lightning came in a series of flashes and she saw the girl standing on the porch with her face pointed toward the sky and one hand balled into a fist and pressed against her cheek and then just as quickly as the storm had risen the storm was gone. The thunder hushed and the wind died and the lightning retreated.

Cara watched the girl. She was only a figure of gray now and Cara could not see her features and could not see her eyes but she felt the girl looking back at her. Her longdrawn stare like some weapon. Cara stood in the road awash with wonder and she waited for something else to happen but she did not want to move or speak. She only wanted to let the girl steer the moment and the girl was doing just that by holding still.

Cara did not move and the girl did not move and then nature's hush was broken with the call of a whippoorwill and as if that was her signal, the girl lowered her hands to her sides and turned around and disappeared inside the house.

48

Behind the storm, the dark began to lessen. The clouds grew thin and pulled apart like tufts of cotton and star-blinks appeared in the spaces in between and then began to disappear one by one. Cara crossed the yard to the house and looked inside and the girl was lying on the sofa. Asleep again. Or pretending to be that way.

Cara returned to the chair on the porch. She stared blankly and made every excuse for what she had seen. Excuses to support it and excuses to reject it. She grew desperate for Keal to return as her mind raced toward them being somewhere else. There would come a time when she would ask the girl with more emphasis if it was true what they said about her even though she realized there was no answer that would satisfy. She had been delivered to the dogma that we are at the mercy of the world and it was a world that offered no explanations and she had the bent fingers to prove it. And she had seen enough blood in recent days to understand that as long as others assumed the child had a gift from the Almighty then the child was a gateway into those explanations and she would always be hunted.

Cara stood from the chair. She tried to shake it off. Time rushing toward first light. It would have been simple enough for Keal to go and get the money and abandon them and run from the madness and she wasn't sure she could blame him for doing such a thing. But she hoped it wasn't true. Headlights approached and she forgot the thoughts of betrayal and she waited for the big car but these were different headlights. A hand waving from the window as the car passed. She walked out into the yard and she looked around and even in the last remaining veil of night she could envision the arrival of spring though it was months of winter away. But she knew that when it came the blackened ground would turn to green and there would be wildflowers with tiny pink and white petals and the azaleas would recover and pop with blossoms and nature would remove any semblance of what had happened here. In the same way that she had worked to rid the inside of the house of what had happened here. The images of rebirth gave her the unanticipated desire for her and the girl to stay right here but then she heard Wanetah's voice and the echo of the last thing the old woman had said to her before she was taken into care and driven away.

Can you keep her from the edge of the world?

Yes, she thought. I can. And that is not possible here.

The old woman knew something. Cara did not understand what that was. But she believed that Wanetah knew something in the way that birds know where to fly and the snake knows where to slither and the earth knows how to spin. Something that was just there and Cara thought now that the woman's dementia had set that special knowledge free, uninhibited from the constraints of reason or doubt or what you can touch or see.

A chill came over her and she folded her arms and hugged herself. She looked again into the sky and the diminishing darkness. She walked to the road and she looked in the direction that Keal would come from and there was only the dark and empty treelined stretch. She began walking along the road as if her presence there may conjure the big car and then before the sun found the horizon the three of them would be on their way but nothing moved and no headlights appeared and she stopped. Already doubting what she had seen the girl perform against the flashes of lightning and whip of the wind. Something in her giving up as the hill country shifted into blue.

She turned around and walked back to the house and she was going to get the girl and tell her it was time. Time to go. Stepping inside she flipped the lightswitch and there was a man standing in the corner of the room with a badly bandaged neck and claw marks on his face and rips in the sleeves of his leather coat. She gasped when she saw him and he said I don't know what you thought was going to happen that was different from this.

49

Keal stood on the levee and watched the smoke rise from the burning bar and disappear into the outer darkness. He had been alone and felt alone so often in his life that he had found a grim solace in the feeling but as he stood there surrounded by swamp and muck he felt more solitary than he had since the day he buried his mother. Exhausted in mind and body as if the sleepless years had finally declared him the loser in the fight. He watched the sky and imagined that we all turn to smoke and drift away into a neverending blue, removed from voice or judgment. Every man and woman and child. All creatures great and small. A day of ash that would be tender and peaceful and carry us away as weightless as dust.

He had been standing there for an hour, gripped with indecision. Watching the storm move away. Waiting for the new light that was now seeping into the horizon and there was the choice between driving off into solitude or driving off with Cara and the girl and whatever came with that. He closed his eyes and he could see the three of them hundreds of miles away in a stopsign town where little moved and little was questioned and he could sense a time when he would end up loving one or both of them and that was the last fucking thing he wanted. Because when they were caught up to and he was certain they would be caught up to in weeks or months or years then there would be blood and the blood of love flowed darker. And then he thought of the old woman and her appearance and the feeling when he looked up from the fire and saw her that she was some throughline to the other side and these last days had only strengthened the feeling. There was nothing to question, only follow.

He removed the crucifix from around his neck and he knelt and stabbed it into the ground. A makeshift gravesite for Burdean. Maybe for him. And then one day if the water didn't rise over the levee then someone would come upon the crucifix and be left to wonder who put it there and what it was for and then without knowing it the discoverer would have played their own part.

He stood and took one more look toward the smoke against the dawn. I am right where I am supposed to be and if it's going to hurt then it's going to hurt. And he tried to see it all. A future where they were safe. Maybe I can dream it, he thought. Maybe I can see them coming. At least once or twice. At least enough to give us a chance. Maybe that is your answer for how to survive. Maybe. This was the word that he kept repeating as he backed the big car across the levee and onto the road. And that was the word he kept repeating as he drove back toward Cara's house. Resolved to this new life. Rushing to beat the light.

DAWN

50

The girl sat up on the sofa. Wayman leaned on a shotgun like a walking cane and he raised it and directed Cara to sit down next to the girl. He moved around in front of them, the methodical creature of a nightmare, ragged and stained bandage around his neck and with scratches on his pitted face and the longeyed look of the ruined. He held the shotgun with slumped shoulders as if carrying a heavy weight and a trail of blood ran from a cut on the back of his hand and down his pinky finger and dripped onto the floor.

"This is fairly insulting," he said.

The girl leaned over close to Cara on the sofa and Cara put her arm around her.

"Don't you want to know what is fairly insulting?" he said.

"No."

He tipped the shotgun barrel to the floor and stood it upright and rested his hand on the butt. She thought the way he had moved across the room was his sardonic gait but she could see now that he was weak.

"Well," he said. "I will tell you. It is insulting that you would come back here and sit around like there was nothing in the world to cause you a shred of concern."

"I'm not concerned."

"That explains it then."

He took two steps backward and let his back fall against the wall. Dragging the muzzle across the floor. The dustblue dawn fell into the windows and she knew if Keal was coming then he was coming soon. Wayman's head hung and his slick hair fell across his face and stuck to the bloodstreaks of the claw marks and his eyes seemed to retreat deep into their sockets. He coughed once and then leaned over to spit out blood.

"Move your arm from her," he said.

"Why didn't you wind the watch?"

"The watch?"

"Yes. We found it next to the wolf. It is yours?"

"You could say that."

"So why didn't you wind it or fix it?"

He laughed a little. Coughed again and spit again. When Cara did not move her arm from around the girl he tapped the muzzle on the floor.

"Move your arm and scoot away from her."

When she did not move again he lifted the shotgun inches from the floor and pulled the trigger and blew a fractured hole in the hardwood. Cara and the girl shrunk down into the sofa with the blast. He pumped the gun and the shell bounced at his feet and then he raised the shotgun to them and a twist of smoke curled around the muzzle. The sound of the shot seemed to awaken him. His head lifted and his eyes came full and his posture straightened.

"Where is it?"

"Where is what?"

"My watch."

She shrugged.

"I don't guess it matters where it is. I don't guess it matters if you move away from her like I'm telling you to do. It's not going to change anything. Time will be time. The end will be the end. And so forth and so on."

"I know you," Cara said.

"You don't know me."

"I do. I've seen you."

"You saw me through the window when I stood with the flames."

"No."

"No?"

"I know you from somewhere else."

"Everybody knows everybody from somewhere else. We're all one person. We all love and hate and bitch and moan. We all think we do it different but we don't. You know me and I know you."

The bleeding had become more pronounced through the bandage. A steady drain from the wolf wounds in the back of his neck, darkening his throat and chest. He took a sidestep as if a little drunk but then he regained his balance. He took two deep breaths as if to reset himself.

"Now," he said. "Get away from her. And little girl, get up and come over here. We got some walking to do."

"You won't make it," Cara said.

He raised the shotgun and blasted a hole in the ceiling, a small explosion of drywall and insulation spraying across Cara and the girl.

"Haven't you shot my house enough?"

"Enough."

"Yes. Enough."

"Everyone always thinks something is enough. Or not enough. So we spin around and around," he said. Then he suddenly dropped to one knee. He balanced the shotgun on his thigh, pointed at them.

"You're not the same," she said.

"The same as what?"

"As anything I've ever seen. Taking her won't start the hands of the watch. Taking her won't stop your blood from flowing out of your body. What you don't know is that taking her won't change anything."

He lowered his eyes to the floor. His breathing labored. A drop of sweat fell from the end of his nose and tapped on the floor. He then raised his eyes back to Cara as if he had just come to some divine realization.

"What you don't know is that taking her changes everything."

He then rose from his knee and he leveled the barrel on Cara but he didn't fire as they were interrupted by the sound of the road and the rumble of the big car. Wayman turned his attention to see the headlight shining up the rutted drive. He stepped behind the halfwall separating the rooms and he told them both to keep their mouths shut or be the first to go.

Keal parked behind the Volkswagen and killed the ignition. The creak of the car door opening. The thump of it closing. Cara and the girl sat on the sofa with their eyes toward the door and the barrel of the shotgun was pointed at them from behind the halfwall and when Keal's bootheels hit the floor he saw them on the sofa and then he saw the holes in the floor and the ceiling and he jerked the pistol from his belt as Wayman stepped out and they fired together as if in agreement, Keal missing and Wayman hitting Keal and knocking him backward, Keal tripping on the doorjamb and tumbling back out of the doorway.

Wayman moved across the threshold and looked down at Keal. He was writhing in pain and clutching at his side, the pistol fallen from his hand and out of reach. Wayman pumped the shotgun and stood over Keal and Keal looked up at him. He did not bother to raise his hand in some useless defense and he did not bother to speak. He laid his head back onto the porch slab and waited for the sound and the sound did not arrive with the boom of finality but it arrived in a crack. After the crack there was a moment of suspension as Wayman's eyes opened wide in the shock of sudden knowledge. And then the shotgun fell from his hands and his lanky frame went slack and he folded like a marionette at Keal's feet. Cara was standing there behind him with the hammer. The hammer that she had snatched from the windowsill and driven into the back of his head.

EPILOGUE

In the casual eye of the passerby they could have been a family. A mother and a father and a daughter going about the immediate workings of life. The woman's hair was now the same color as the darkhaired girl's and the man walked with a limp from a badly treated wound just above his hip. At first glance the limp was what kept him walking behind the woman and the girl whenever they were at the grocery store or along the sidewalk. The woman and the girl shared a language and casual nature with one another and the man moved in and out of that but remained on the periphery, unwilling to intrude. He stood behind them or away from them and when he did move closer there was the exchange of only a few words and then he would move away again as if the woman and the girl had given him some furtive message and he was looking for the person to deliver it to.

It was a nomadic existence, moving from town to town every few weeks. In and out of motels. Sometimes a short-term apartment with stained carpet and the stench of cigarettes. Keal limping along and finding cash jobs stacking boxes or shoveling mulch into truck beds or cleaning bathrooms nobody else was willing to clean. Cara doing the same, offering to work for tips only in roadside cafés or beer joints in exchange for no questions asked which was always a much easier agreement than she anticipated. There was a simplicity to their routine and pattern to the rules they had made for themselves that offered both satisfaction and anxiety. One moment believing they were playing the game the right way and in other moments overcome with the dread that they were simply being lured into the falsehood of safety and there would be a rush from the shadows in the hour of greatest calm.

The girl was the only one of them who slept. Keal could not and Cara could not. Their sleep came in intervals, sporadic and unpredictable and they moved around one another in the night as if changing shifts, taking turns with the television or taking turns going for walks along the dark streets of whatever small town they were hiding in. Sometimes in their passing they would sit together and mindlessly stare at the screen or make suggestions of what to do next, their conversation confined to the basics. Neither asking the questions they wanted to ask, knotted by the fear of letting go and finding something in the other person that would then be snatched away. The hesitance of the scarred.

The weeks turned into months and they shifted towns through the bleakness of winter and the rains of spring and the oppression of summer and then when the season returned to fall and the colors began to transform they began to talk to one another about more than the next move during the empty hours of night. The cool autumn breeze signaling a year since this odyssey had begun and it blew into their open windows like the wind of permission. She wanted to know about his dreams and he told her about all of them he could remember and admitted that he didn't have them anymore. He told her about his mother. How tough she was. How good she was. She told him about Lola and showed him the lock of hair. He wanted to know if she knew where Lola was and Cara said no. When the time felt right he asked again about her fingers and she told him about the night she came home with the man from her past waiting in her yard and the hours that followed and she told the story with more honesty than she expected. She spoke of the agony of not being able to question him. Ask him why and how he came to that decision. And then she would say she didn't want to know. They both questioned the nature of fate and they both believed they were gripped in its clutches because neither of them could find any other way to explain their being together.

They exchanged tales of childhood and tried to figure out if they somehow had known any of the same people and revealed favorite movies and songs and in those moments there was a great exhale between them as if they were not the hunted but only two people who had chosen to be with one another. They always ended up talking about the girl and Keal admitted how closely he watched her when there was a thunderstorm or when the tornado siren wailed, trying to see something in her actions or in her eyes that would reveal the miracle in a way he could both believe in and understand. He asked Cara if she did the same and she said yes and that she had tried to talk to the girl about her hinted abilities and the girl would never give her an answer but only a suggestion. And when they spoke of the girl the conversation always ended with a dumbstruck silence. As if the things they had seen and had to consider simply could not be real. As if the things they had done could not be real. They were both killers. They were both fugitives. They were both risking it all for a child who seemed to have been delivered out of a biblical tale. But neither one of them raised any doubt as to the road that had been chosen.

Sometimes when they sat close to one another and talked through the darkness Cara would lean and touch her shoulder to his and sometimes Keal would do the same. Sometimes it was the brush of a leg. Neither would move away when the touch was made, the small and pleasurable measures of affection that seemed to be enough for them to make it through until the morning blue. And though neither would admit it to the other while they shared the night with the girl sleeping safely, both had begun to consider the idea that with the length of time that had passed, they might be separating themselves from whatever malevolence they had survived.

They were both wrong.

In the middle of a night when Cara was washing dishes and busing tables at a twentyfour hour diner, Keal woke in alarm from a brief and striking nightmare. The first distressing dream in months. He was sweating and confused and he swung his arms around in the blackness to fend off some unseen enemy and when he finally managed to calm himself and realize where he was he could hear the steady beat of a drum like the heartbeat of the dark. They were living on the fringe of town limits, in a three-room apartment on the second floor of what had once been a furniture factory. A stripped down dwelling with woodplank floors and concrete walls. Somewhere down in Louisiana. Cara and the girl shared one bedroom and he was in the other.

He wiped his face with his hands and measured his breath and then he got up from the bed and walked into the shared room. He opened the door of the other bedroom to check on the girl and she was not there. He then looked at the front door and it was cracked open and he hurried over and pulled it open and the girl was standing there with her hands on the railing and looking across the night. In the pose of being called to attention.

Her eyes were fixed on the lights and the sounds coming from the parking lot that decades before had been filled with the vehicles of factory employees. But now the lot was filled with spotlights and generators and moving trucks and trailers. In the middle of it all stood a whitetop tent with a bloodred cross painted on the top. Workers moved in and out of the moving trucks, rolling out sound equipment and stacks of chairs and more essentials for the traveling spectacle of revival. A black hearse was parked off to the side with its engine running and headlights on. Beneath the grand tent the stage had just been assembled and two men worked to erect a pulpit at the front of the stage while at the back of the stage a man sat at a drum kit and stomped the kickdrum in a hard and steady beat. Like some ageless and rhythmic announcement to all of those who could hear the thumping that Jesus had arrived and the wicked never rest.

Keal and the girl were watching the commotion when he saw the headlights of the Volkswagen approaching in the distance and he did not need to wait for Cara to arrive for him to know that she had felt the same thing he had felt when he was roused from the rough and restless nightmare. It was time to go. Keal looked back across the lot and toward the tent and his eyes fell on the bloodred cross. He stood still and grew hypnotized as he imagined the cross losing shape and turning to blood and the crimson beginning to run in streams down the tent and drip from its edges and he imagined the crowd who would gather tomorrow and stand beneath the blooddrips with their hands open and their mouths open as they celebrated their own deliverance into a life beyond sin and hate as if it was something they could wash clean in the runoff of the parking lot temple. The drumbeat thrummed and the blood ran and the spotlights stared back at him with big white eyes. We see you. We see you. The crowd dancing in the blood and the shouts of jubilation and the vigorous energy from the pulpit as the preacher powered through the performance that could have been inspired by either sin or salvation and Keal saw it all and he felt the hands of proclamation reaching around his throat and reaching around the throats of Cara and the girl and dragging them back into the lightless cellar and when the girl reached over and touched his hand he jerked and jumped as if he himself had been electrocuted by the lifethrust of hardnosed religion.

Before first light, before the sun rose and before the chairs were in place and the offering baskets were ready to be filled and before the first hallelujah was spoken and before the first souls were saved, they were gone. Carrying with them no trust or certainty in the world other than what they could give to one another.

ACKNOWLEDGMENTS

My thanks to the Patterson family, to Burns Strider, and to the teams at Trident Media Group, No Exit Press, Éditions Gallmeister, and Little, Brown and Company. And as always to Ellen Levine and Josh Kendall for embracing my stories, and to my girls for all their support.

ABOUT THE AUTHOR

MICHAEL FARRIS SMITH is an award-winning writer whose novels have appeared on Best of the Year lists with *Esquire;* NPR; *Southern Living; Garden & Gun; O, The Oprah Magazine; Book Riot;* and numerous other outlets, and have been named Indie Next, Barnes & Noble Discover, and Amazon Best of the Month selections. As a screenwriter, he scripted the feature-film adaptations of his novels *Desperation Road* and *The Fighter,* titled for the screen as *Rumble Through the Dark.* With his band MFS & The Smokes, Smith wrote and released the record *Lostville,* which was produced by Grammy nominee Jimbo Mathus. He lives in Oxford, Mississippi, with his wife and daughters.